Outstanding Pı

MW01679038

"A damned good writer."—Davi
Flight, *Critical Mass*, and some 7

"*Strong Conviction* is a good crime story with interesting characters and solid writing. Trevor Scott weaves a web of small-town controversy that entraps our hero...with vivid description he paints characters who breathe and sets up believable conflict."—*Pine Bluff* (Arkansas) *Commercial*

"*Strong Conviction*...a first class shocker fully developed with crystalline and lively dialogue, adroit pacing, and commanding characters who find themselves enmeshed in extraordinary and often deadly circumstances, with the right mix of potent romantic interest."—*Scribesworld*

"Mr. Scott brings his powerful and prestigious experience into play with his newest thriller, *Hypershot*. Mr. Scott utilizes his usual arsenal of literary techniques to build *Hypershot* into a first-class thriller: pacing, effective love interests, compelling characters finding themselves in unusual and deadly circumstances, clear and effective dialogue, and just plain thrilling circumstances. His settings are reminiscent of James Bond. A great fourth book!"—*The Midwest Book Review*

"Previous titles have fit the Tom Clancy techno mold, but this topical tale of DNA research and a possible cure for heart disease falls more in the James Bond tradition of fancy cars and fast women."—*Publishers Weekly*, on *The Dolomite Solution*

"Trevor Scott delivers with *The Dolomite Solution*. Scott ratchets up the action. He is an expert at thoroughly deceiving the reader, drawing us into a seemingly insolvable plot just as he fascinates us with action that is non-stop...a wonderful read."—*The Midwest Book Review*

"Scott has the high-tech jargon down pat...he takes readers around the world for a thrill-packed adventure. Technothriller fans looking for an alternative to Clancy will find Scott a somewhat smaller-scale but perhaps even more authentic alternative."—*Booklist* on *Extreme Faction*

"Trevor Scott's action-packed post-Cold War spy thriller is certainly that-a thriller. *Extreme Faction* takes the reader around the world, into different cultures, lifestyles and ideals with flawless ease. I'd recommend this adventure highly."

—*Duluth News-Tribune*

"*Extreme Faction* is fast-paced, realistic, and more than a bit frightening."—*Statesman Journal*, Salem, Oregon

"*Extreme Faction* is a thrill-packed, non-stop, absolutely riveting action/adventure, novel from first page to last."

—*The Midwest Book Review*

"As much fun as a Bruce Willis action movie."

—*Rocket eNewsletter* on *Extreme Faction*

"A great read. A roller coaster ride of murder, espionage and intrigue."—David Hagberg, author of *High Flight*

"*Fatal Network* is a masterfully written, splendidly executed, superb thriller."—*The Midwest Book Review*

"This is a thriller with some real thrills, an adventure with new ideas, and an espionage drama firmly rooted in the convoluted realities of modern Europe. A real gut-buster of a thriller."

—*Statesman Journal*, Salem, Oregon

"Unique twists and turns...a deadly cat and mouse game."

—*Duluth News-Tribune*

VITAL FORCE

Also by Trevor Scott

Fatal Network
Extreme Faction
The Dolomite Solution
Hypershot
Strong Conviction
The Dawn of Midnight

VITAL FORCE

Trevor Scott

Salvo Press
Beaverton, Oregon

VITAL FORCE

Salvo Press
P.O. Box 7396
Beaverton, OR 97007
www.salvopress.com

Library of Congress Control Number: 2005937392

ISBN: 1-930486-59-6

Printed in the United States of America

First Edition

April 2006

Visit the author at: www.trevorscott.com

For my siblings
Chuck, Sue, Deb, Jeff, Gina, Greg, Jill and Steph

Acknowledgments

Thanks to all of the readers who have taken a chance and purchased one of my books. A special thanks to those who have passed the word and recommended one of my titles to a friend or relative. I am indebted to the kind people of China who always had a smile for me and my family. I hope to return there soon.

Thanks also to all of the dedicated Air Force personnel and the defense contractors who are working on the airborne and ground-based laser systems that will soon protect our country from rogue state ICBMs.

PROLOGUE

Volgograd, Soviet Union

The metal bar smashed against the side of his head, knocking Jake Adams to his knees, the wooden chair still lashed to his naked back. His face landed with a thud on the wet, moldy pavement, his eyelashes fluttering in a puddle of his own blood as his eyeballs swirled around trying to focus on anything. Anything that would let Jake know he was still alive.

"We can stop any time, Adams," came the harsh, Slavic voice that Jake had learned to hate over the past two weeks. "Just tell us what we need to know."

Jake shifted his shoulders and tried to lift his head from the cold floor. The taste of iron from his blood seeped through his teeth as he swallowed. He couldn't last much longer like this. He had eaten only stale bread and drank only filthy water during his stay along the Volga River-captured and brought to this dungeon-like basement after only two days in the city that had, until twenty-some years before, been known as Stalingrad. Over fourteen days he had thought he was losing his mind, envisioning ghosts of some three million people who had died during the Nazi siege and eventual surrender. Apparitions of his mind, he was sure, but in that dank cell he currently called home, he could almost hear the screams of horror and cries of pain from those killed in that war. Maybe the screams were his own, echoing off the thick stone walls.

The Soviet GRU officer, dressed in civilian clothes, shoved the metal bar under Jake's chin and pressed down against his wind pipe, bringing instant pain and cutting off his air.

Jake's mind spun as he gasped for breath. He had to hold out. He couldn't tell them anything. His cover story placed him in Volgograd promoting a communications company that did not exist. At least not in any real sense. Sure the Company had offices in Baltimore and Munich, where Jake reportedly worked. But it was all a front set up by the CIA. That's what his captors suspected and what Jake had to never confirm. Yet, he knew that at this very moment the offices in both cities would be wiped clean and cleared out like a speakeasy one step ahead of the Feds. Only a few knew Jake's real mission in Volgograd, and all would deny any knowledge of the same.

Struggling against the bar at his throat, Jake lifted his chin. His brutal captor let up on the metal bar. Jake coughed and spit up blood. Recovering, he said, "You know, Ivan, you need to work a little on your people skills." He coughed again, trying to catch his breath and waiting for the next blow. His ribs were broken, his shoulder separated, and he was sure he had a fractured skull. He wished they would get it over with and kill him. The pain would end. Another part of him, that with a desire to beat these bastards at their own game, wanted nothing more than to last until their hands were blistered.

Suddenly, the heavy metal door burst open and Jake could see a couple sets of legs. Uniforms. Then muffled Russian. If his left ear drum hadn't burst from a blow two days ago, he could have understood what they were saying.

Hands grasped under Jake's arms and pulled him to a sitting position on his chair. His eyes focused on the man he had called Ivan for the past two weeks standing at the door about to leave. "Have a nice day," Jake mumbled.

Disgusted, the GRU officer left and slammed the door in his wake.

Shifting his head to his left, Jake's eyes finally settled on a man in a Soviet uniform. Something wasn't right, though. The man was wearing the uniform of the Soviet Missile Forces. A captain.

Jake looked closer at the man's face. "Yuri?" He barely got the name out before he felt himself sliding forward, his mind reeling.

Then came the blackness.

CHAPTER 1

Fifteen Years Later
Khabarovsk Province, Russia

Isolated in the taiga of the Russian Far East, among the thick pines and rolling hills, the mobile SS-27 missile sat atop the transporter erector launcher, camouflaged in forest green and brown that made it blend into its surroundings. The launcher slowly rose into firing position.

Back in the snowy forest some hundred meters, the darkness of night did not allow a view of the launcher by the forty heavily-armed soldiers huddled in fox holes.

The crew inside the mobile launch facility had only the view on their video monitors from cameras strapped to trees, and even those were grainy and obscured somewhat by the green from the night vision optics.

Jake Adams watched as each crewman prepared for the launch. He was the only American in the box, sent to observe the launch as part of a cooperative exchange. And he was still wondering why he was there, since he was no longer with the Air Force or the American Intelligence Network, the two-year-old agency that combined the CIA, FBI, NSA, ATF, DEA, and, like the cancer it had become, nearly every other acronym in the U.S. government. He had never officially worked for the AIN, having at one time been with the former CIA, but he had been called back on occasion to help the Network. This assignment had come about by request from an old Soviet officer, Yuri Pushkina, whom he had met in the Ukraine while verifying the destruction of intermediate-range nuclear missiles in the late '80s. And again in Volgograd.

Now, Jake watched his old friend, a colonel in the Russian Missile

Forces, pace nervously from station to station while he awaited the launch command from the central command authority outside of Moscow, some three thousand miles to the west. The colonel's plodding gate brought images in Jake's mind of a bull stamping back and forth, hoping to catch a bullfighter off guard.

The facility itself was stuffed beyond capacity. Normally there would have been a man at each end of the box-like control room that resembled a small European truck trailer lined with communications equipment. Each of the launch officers was separated by distance, just like the American crews, to make it nearly impossible to fire the missiles without at least the collusion of two dedicated officers simultaneously turning their launch keys. Beyond them, a half a dozen enlisted men manned other consoles. All were dressed in forest camouflage jump suits.

The extra observers, like Jake and a couple of other dignitaries, made the walls seem to close in on them. The red lights and glow from the green luminescent static-free floor gave the small room an eerie atmosphere.

"Why so nervous?" Jake asked the colonel.

Yuri shrugged his broad shoulders, the boards on his impeccable dress uniform rising. "I don't know." He put his arm around Jake's shoulder and pulled him aside. "You remember outside Kiev, before the hoist dropped and nearly broke the case on that nuke? I had a feeling inside my stomach. Something was wrong. I have same feeling."

It was strange for Jake to hear this dedicated and highly-decorated Cold Warrior admit that he had gut feelings about anything, and especially something this important. "Sounds like you just want everything to go right, Yuri. Nothing wrong with that. What'll they do, send you to Siberia?"

That got a laugh from Yuri, who had grown up in central Siberia, and any assignment east or west of his homeland would have been considered cushy.

"You see," Yuri said. "That's why I wanted you here." The tall, strong man lifted his square chin and went back to looking over the shoulders of his men.

Twenty minutes now from the scheduled launch time. Jake checked his watch and hoped his advice was correct. The SS-27 was a newer weapon. This launch had only been scheduled after the last test, two months ago, had resulted in the missile exploding in its launcher. They were testing a new guidance system, using only the SS-27 three-stage rocket. Everything else was new. In fact, if this test went as planned, the Russians would destroy an entire class of long-range intercontinental ballistic missiles. It was a modernization of the force that Washington, London and Paris all agreed was necessary, and that Moscow had found money for by oil sales to those three countries. The one stipulation from the Western nations had been an observer at each step of the way. Independent observers with no current affiliation with any government.

North Pacific, Sea of Okhotsk

Flying at 36,000 feet, the Boeing 747, painted black as the night, cruised north along the Kamchatka Peninsula, just outside Russian international airspace.

Monitoring a console in what would have been the upper first class section, Colonel Tim Powers glanced sideways at a major from his new command. Colonel Powers had been a Cold War missile officer, spending twenty-four hour shifts hunkered down deep underground in launch facilities in North Dakota and Wyoming. Later, as he gained rank, he had transferred to Space Command, a post that he thought would bring his first star.

"How far from the Russian coast?" the colonel asked the flight crew over his mic.

"Right on our flight plan, Sir," came the voice of the pilot, Captain Billy Waters, with a strong Georgia accent. "We're banking west now and will start turning south in exactly ten minutes. Still in international airspace."

"Thanks, Billy." The colonel shifted nervously in his chair and glanced about the compartment at his fellow officers. All of them had been handpicked by Colonel Powers, not only for their high compartmentalized security clearances, but for their ability to keep their mouth shut at the "O" Club with their fellow officers.

Although the Russians knew they were there, and, in fact, had encouraged their observing presence, they also had no idea of their true mission. Had they known, they would have scrambled MIGs and shot them from the sky. If they could. The colonel smiled thinking about that possible encounter. Would they be able to counter those air-to-air missiles? They had done it repeatedly with American Sidewinders, so there was no reason to believe their success would be any less effective with inferior Russian missiles.

"Heading south," the pilot said.

The large plane started a slow bank to the left.

They were close now. Time to test the true capabilities of this bird, the colonel thought.

"COIL up and ready?" the colonel asked.

"Check."

"Yes, Sir."

"All right, folks. Let's prepare for the launch." He checked his watch, which was synchronized to nuclear time down to a hundredth of a second. "Five minutes, twenty two seconds."

The colonel checked each of his crew. They were determined, their eyes intense and focused on their screens. They were about to commit a breech of international law, but that didn't seem to bother any of them. If all went as planned, missiles would become as innocuous as the bow and arrow. He smiled. Welcome to modern warfare.

♦

Inside the Russian launch facility, the men made last-minute preparations. Jake knew the trailer was nearly soundproof, but he still considered plugging his ears during the launch. He had observed a number of ground-launched cruise missile launches at Vandenburg Air Force Base, California, in the '80s, and they had been a lot louder than he would have thought-especially while outside and a short distance away.

Watching his old friend and sometime adversary, Jake could sense a high level of angst and uncertainty in the man. Something he would have never guessed possible in Yuri Pushkina.

Yuri waved Jake over to a console that would show the flight path of the modified SS-27 Topol-M missile.

"Here we go, my friend," Yuri said. "Ten seconds."

Jake and Yuri watched the computer monitor over the shoulder of a young captain. As the time counted off, the first indication that they had a launch was not on the computer, but the slight shaking felt throughout the compartment and the muffled roar from outside. Then the missile showed progress on the computer screen, climbing to three times the speed of sound toward the northeast in just seconds. Jake knew that the missile would swiftly reach a speed of 24,000 kilometers per hour in a few minutes. At that rate, with a nuclear payload, the missile would be able to strike Seattle in thirty minutes and Los Angeles in less than forty.

Hell of a deal, Jake thought, watching the computer screen, as the missile reached a trajectory passing over the Tatar Straight and Sakhalin Island. Soon, the missile would reach critical velocity and altitude over the Sea of Okhotsk, pass over the Kamchatka Peninsula before the planned self destruction over the Bering Sea, where a Russian sub would mark the reentry and ensure nothing remained on the surface. Which was unlikely, Jake knew, considering the speed of descent and the destructive charge.

Yuri leaned forward toward the screen as the missile started to cross the Sea of Okhotsk.

Then it happened. The unlikely. The improbable. Suddenly, the computer image that signified the missile disappeared.

"What the hell?" Yuri yelled in Russian. "What happened, Captain Petrov?"

The young captain clicked a few keys on his computer, desperately trying to make the missile re-appear. Nothing. He shook his head in disbelief. "It is gone, Colonel Pushkina."

The next few minutes were chaos as secure phones rang from superiors and Yuri tried his best to explain that he had no idea what had happened.

CHAPTER 2

The Asian woman watched the city of Khabarovsk pass by through the passenger window, her mind muddled by nearly twenty-four hours of constant travel. She had read in an on-flight magazine that Khabarovsk was the eastern gateway to Russia, serviced by an international airport and two main rail lines, including the Trans-Siberian Railroad. The city was mostly planted along the eastern side of the massive Amur River, a major supply route for trade with Japan and a magnet for summer sun worshippers. Now, though, with winter still holding on, the 615,000 citizens of Khabarovsk spent most of their time at work, huddled at home, or in the smoky bars, she guessed.

The Volkswagen Santana sedan cruised through the darkness along Lenina Street, only a few other cars in sight, and those creeping along like snails.

She gazed at the driver, who tapped chop sticks on the dash in sync with the Beatles song, Tax Man. Watching the street lights come on, her only thoughts were on the absurd man to her left. The man she only knew as Laughing Dragon. From what she had seen in the last six months, the man lived up to both parts of his moniker. She understood the Dragon part, since she had seen the man turn on enemies with vicious precision without breaking a sweat-the only thing missing was the fire from his mouth. It was the Laughing part that had so baffled her. He would break into an insidious unrestrained titter for no apparent reason, bringing a chill to her skin. Perhaps he was as insane as her former runner had said just before he turned up missing.

"Tax Man," the driver sang, his voice much higher than the Beatle, his chop sticks clanking the dash, and his bald head bobbing up and down.

"There's Komsomolsk Square," the woman said, trying to get him back on track to their goal.

The driver yelled "Tax Man" one more time and then broke into a high-pitched cackle-his version of a laugh.

"Komsomolsk Square," the woman repeated, pointing now for emphasis.

Laughing Dragon pulled the car to the side of the road and shut down the engine. He turned his head toward her and his smile washed away. "You ever interrupt the Beatles again, Li. . . you know what. Zai jian."

She knew. Two months ago in Shanghai, outside a warehouse along the shipping docks, a contact had told him to shut his mouth when the Laughing Dragon had erupted into a guffaw at the man for slipping on wet pavement. She had never seen the Dragon escape so quickly. Zai jian. Goodbye to the man.

She bowed her head to him. "Wo dong. I understand."

"Good. Let's go."

The two of them got out and headed across the square toward the river. By the time they reached the edge of the square and crossed the snowy park to the edge of the river, darkness had set in completely over this part of Russia-a place that reminded Li more of Manchuria.

Laughing Dragon stopped suddenly, his hand on her arm. "We talk English," he said to her. "More preciously, I talk English."

"Precisely," she corrected.

"Exactly. How else I learn words meaning to Abby Road album?"

Always back to the Beatles, she thought.

Further up the river a figure appeared from behind some pine trees, his hulking figure a silhouette against the industrial skyline across the river.

Laughing Dragon pulled Li forward.

"Close enough," came a harsh voice, heavily accented, followed by a gloved hand extended outward.

The two of them stopped, the only sound the soft flow of water rippling against a pile of rocks on the river's edge. She knew nothing of the man. That was out of necessity, as always. He was Russian. That's all she knew. From five meters she could not see his face.

"What go up must come down," Laughing Dragon said.

"Only if someone shoots it down," the Russian said.

Coded pleasantries over, the Russian slid his hand inside his wool coat and extracted what appeared to be a bundle wrapped in plastic. He threw the package and it landed at the feet of Laughing Dragon, who reached down for it.

"Wait," the man in the shadows said. "Wait until I go. Everything is there." With that, the man backed behind the pines and was not seen again.

Poor tactics, she thought.

Laughing Dragon glanced at her. "You think he not very smart?"

"We could have had another person up the river," she said.

He let out a more subdued laugh and then pointed at a red dot bouncing around Li's chest. "And we both die here in Khabarovsk on bank of river."

She looked around trying to find the source of the red dot, knowing she would be dead before she heard the sound if the shooter dared to pull the trigger.

Her boss reached down for the bundle and then nodded for them to head back toward the car.

"Why not open the package?" she said, looking around for the red dot.

"It there. It always there. If not, it be last time."

They shuffled across the square to the car. Once inside, Laughing Dragon opened the package. There was a stack of American dollars, a series of photos, and instructions in English. Which was one reason she had been called in. Her boss could speak English, but his reading was limited to children's books. He shoved the bills inside his jacket and handed her the instructions.

She looked them over, memorized her part, and then set the paper on the seat next to her. Although she had just gotten off a flight from San Francisco that morning, catching a connecting flight from Beijing, she now saw she would be heading back to America as soon as she could catch a return flight. She would have to push her contact there. Hurry him into something she knew would include more gratuitous sex. Although that repulsed her, she knew the reward would be well worth the unpleasantness. But first she would have to work here with Laughing Dragon.

♦

Hours later, twenty miles southeast of the missile test site, in a bar on the outskirts of Khabarovsk, Jake Adams leaned back in his chair and poured another shot of vodka down his throat, Yuri Pushkina doing the same and then both slamming the glass to the table.

Letting out a deep breath, Jake said, “All right, that’s the last one, Yuri.”

The Russian laughed and then his face became serious. “Come on, my friend. This is my retirement.”

Putting his arm around the Russian, Jake whispered, “It wasn’t your fault. They’ll see that.”

Yuri shook his head. “They always find someone to blame for these things.”

“Even so. You’ll have your pension.”

“I could work at McDonald’s in Moscow. I’m sure they hire me.”

Jake glanced about the smoky room, which was crowded mostly with off-duty soldiers and tungsten miners, still dressed in grubby denim overalls. The vodka had set his head spinning, but his old friend would need his counsel and companionship. Jake would have to switch to beer, though. He stopped a waitress and ordered a beer and another shot of vodka.

“I don’t want beer, Jake,” Yuri said to him.

“That’s for me. No more vodka.”

An hour passed. Patrons came and went, but the two of them continued their assault on the Khabarovsk alcohol supply.

Yuri finally moved his chair closer to Jake, put his arm around his neck, and said, “I shouldn’t tell you this.” He hesitated as his eyes shifted about the room. “But I’m sure you already know this. My superiors know what happened to our missile.” He raised his bushy brows and smiled at Jake. It was the same smile he had displayed when Jake awoke in the back of the taxi a the Volgograd airport years ago-Yuri in civilian clothes then and extolling his virtues for saving Jake’s ass.

When Yuri didn’t elaborate, Jake said, “And?”

“And I think you know.” He pulled his arm from Jake, crossed both of them over his thick chest, and then leaned back in his chair.

Jake had no idea what in the hell was going on. “I’m lost, Yuri. I think I’ve had too much to drink.”

“You know!” His voice resonated and brought stares from two young soldiers at the closest table.

Shaking his head, Jake said, “No, I don’t.”

“Your fucking plane.” This time Yuri whispered loudly, his words slurred.

Jake wasn’t sure what in the hell he was talking about. But he was aware of the two soldiers, who were nowhere near their level of inebriation. "Let's get some air, Yuri."

The large Russian started to his feet and his chair slipped out and crashed to the floor, but Yuri recovered before following the chair to the wooden surface.

As the two of them got to the sidewalk, Jake realized that the February air had dipped down toward zero. The Russian leaned up against the brick building and lit a cigarette, bringing the tip to a bright orange.

"What the hell you trying to tell me, Yuri?"

"You know."

"No. I don't."

The man considered him carefully, watching Jake's facial expression. "You don't know, my friend." He sucked on the cigarette, let out a stream of smoke and said, "The stipulation to this test from the Americans was to observe the test from a plane over the Sea of Okhotsk. You know this much?"

"No! Remember, Yuri, you brought me into this. I have nothing to do with the U.S. government. I was here as an independent observer."

The Russian considered this.

Jake was as confused as a child in a physics lecture. He had been living in Innsbruck, Austria, where he had been for the last few years running a private security firm, when he had gotten the call from Yuri, followed by a round-trip airline ticket from Munich to Vladivostok, Russia, and an expedited visa for his passport. Based on his past affiliation with the old CIA, he had been compelled to notify the Network. But that was all he knew.

"My superiors," Yuri said, "have been notified by your government that they shot down the missile. It was all a big joke to them. We make promise to cut our missiles with this new one, and they laugh at us. Spit in our face." He took another hit on his cigarette, his eyes cutting deeply into Jake through the smoke.

"What do you mean they shot it down. With what?"

"They say it was laser. Zap! One shot. Star Wars shit."

Jake had read about the Airborne Laser program, but he had no idea they had become operational. "But why?"

Yuri shrugged his shoulders. "Because they could. It's one thing to test on your missiles, but to shoot down someone else's missile-" His voice trailed off as he stamped out his cigarette on the sidewalk.

Jake imagined the Russian government was hot right now, with that American revelation. Damn! What balls that took.

"Our world is over, Jake. Passed us by. Shit. Laser beams shooting missiles out of the sky. What's the use?"

He had a good point, and maybe that was it. Maybe the Americans had to do it this way.

"There was no other way," Jake said. "You tell someone you can shoot down their nuclear missiles, maybe they believe you, maybe they don't. But you shoot down the most sophisticated missile in their arsenal, and they gotta believe you can do it again and again. The race is over."

"No shit!" Yuri thought for a moment, his eyes seemingly transfixed on something behind Jake, and then returning directly to peer at the brown in the American's eyes. "I need to go. Your friends in the Air Force just made me a dinosaur."

"What will you do, Yuri?"

"I don't know. Maybe Siberia. Go fishing. You come back, Jake. I have a dacha on a lake near here. We go fishing together." The Russian finally smiled. "Thank you for coming here."

Jake helped him into a cab and patted the top as the car drove off. As he walked down the cobblestone in the cold darkness, he couldn't help but think of the missile test earlier in the day. A laser. Man, the world was changing, he thought. Would it make the thousands of ICBMs in both the Russian and U.S. arsenals obsolete? More than likely. It was too much for him to think about with all the alcohol.

♦

The dark Volkswagen sedan pulled away from the curb, its lights off, as it crept along the road a block and a half behind the man on the sidewalk.

In three blocks, the man stumbled up into the lobby of the Shevchenko Hotel, and the car pulled over to the side of the road.

Inside the car, the bald driver tapped his chopsticks lightly against the steering wheel. The Asian woman, her eyes having a hard time staying awake, tried her best to block out the tap tap tapping. If she could find a way out of this, away from this crazy man, she would. But was she really that different from him? Probably not. Not as annoying, she knew that much. Just finish the task at hand, she thought, and then back to America.

CHAPTER 3

There was no way for Jake to tell how long he had been sleeping before it happened. In the darkness of the hotel room, the shades pulled tight against the city lights, his first recollection of anything out of the ordinary came in the form of a slight sound. A clicking noise. But strange hotels always had strange noises, so he closed his eyes again and tried his best to stop the pain in the back of his skull from the vodka.

Next came a struggle, and his spinning mind reeled about as he lashed against the arms and legs that enveloped him. What was that smell? He knew then that he was in trouble.

♦

When he woke again, Jake was cold and shivering in only his underwear and a T-shirt, and obviously in a cramped space. His eyes tried to adjust to the darkness. No way, Jake knew. The odor was unmistakable. Rubber, dirt, oily rags. A car trunk. A car with bad shocks, he thought, as a sudden jerk bounced him up and then back onto the hard surface.

His arms were strapped to his back and something was stretched around his mouth to his neck.

He tried to shift and stretch his legs, but they had run a line from his neck to his hands and then on to his ankles, which were also lashed and wrapped back toward his bound wrists. Someone knew what they were doing, Jake thought. He had done the same to others in the past, and there was no escaping from that kind of binding.

The car turned, rolling him toward his back. A right turn. Then the shocks really started working overtime. A dirt road? A frozen road.

This was no good. What in the hell was going on?

Music and singing. Muffled. Coming from the front. Then the voice was louder. Screaming.

"Back in the U.S.S.R.," the accented voice screeched above the car's engine and the bouncing shocks.

The Beatles? Great! A sadistic Beatles fan.

Suddenly, the car came to a stop. Jake could hear two doors open and the mumbling. What language? Impossible to tell.

When the trunk opened, Jake expected to see light, but all he saw was a dark sky with the occasional star poking out from the swirling clouds.

Both of the dark figures that pulled him out of the trunk wore black ski masks and dark clothing. He noticed they weren't that large, as they struggled to drag him across the snow and set him against the base of a large pine. Jake tried to see the make of car, but it was impossible in that lighting.

"You tell me about missile launch today."

The language was broken and somewhat effeminate.

"You've got me mixed up with someone who gives a shit," Jake said, shifting his body up against the sharp edges of the tree bark. He worked his fingers around the knot in the binding. It wasn't rope. What was it?

The one who had spoken swiftly struck his right foot into Jake's chest, nearly taking his breath away and knocking Jake against the tree.

As Jake recovered, he said, "What the hell was that for?"

"We have all night, Mister Adams. You don't."

Damn, they knew who he was.

"The missile launch. Tell me now!"

"Tell you what?" Jake said, shifting his body up again and trying to shove the material wrapped around his wrists against the sharp bark.

"Tell me about missile."

The clouds spread out and Jake could finally see more stars and more of his two captors.

"What about it? You want a lesson in physics?"

The foot came again. This time from the other person. The boot made contact with his right shoulder, knocking him back against the tree again. An unexpected benefit was that the shot loosened the binding between his feet and hands. He rolled over and started sliding his hands up and down against the bark, trying to cut the line from his hands to his feet.

"We could use lesson in anatomy," the man said, as he pulled out a butterfly knife and flipped it open.

"Hey," Jake said. "Put away the cutlery. What exactly do you want to know about the missile?"

The man kept the knife pointed at Jake. "What happened to missile?"

"Listen. I was just a civilian observer."

Both of them laughed, and Jake finally heard that the second one was more than likely a woman. With the dark bulky clothes, he had not noticed.

"Jake Adams. Air Force Intelligence. CIA. Opened security service in Portland, Oregon. Now operate out of Innsbruck, Austria. Major operations in Italy and Germany. Killed Hungarian agents. Stopped Kurdish plot. Helped Austrian company with new heart disease cure. Want me to tell more?"

"Yeah, you forgot to tell me the last time I got laid."

"Toni Contardo. Six months ago. Just before she was called back into service with the Network." The man burst into a hearty guffaw.

Son of a bitch. They had done their homework. He had thought only the Network knew about his relationship with Toni. He worked harder on his binding now, struggling cautiously.

"So, who the hell are you?" Jake asked them, stalling.

"Tell us about missile and we might let you freeze to death. Otherwise." He waved the knife in the air.

Why should he hold back anything? Jake thought about what Yuri had told him only hours ago. Would it matter if he told these people?

"The missile failed," Jake said. He could have made up any bullshit story. One was as good as the next. "It started to go haywire and the Russians thought it might head toward Kamchatka. They were forced to destroy it."

Two things happened almost simultaneously. The man swished his knife toward Jake and Jake flipped around to his right. The knife slit the binding on his back, freeing his feet, and, unexpectedly, the tie that ran up to his neck. Jake rolled over again and again in the snow as if in pain. Then he sent his right foot into the knee of the approaching man. He heard a crack and the man collapsed in pain, dropping the knife in the snow.

By now, Jake had gotten to his knees. The woman was on him in a hurry, though. Her right foot caught him in the sternum and sent him flying to his back. As she got closer, he caught her legs with a sweep of his leg and sent her to her back. Then he scurried toward her, grabbed the mask covering her head, and, with one smooth motion, pulled it from her head, her long, black hair flopping out in a ponytail.

Damn! A Chinese woman. Gorgeous but shocked. He chopped her in the throat and she rolled over, out of breath.

He had to move now. Jumping to his feet, Jake ran into the forest. His bare feet were freezing, yet he knew he couldn't stop. And those feet would occasionally stumble onto unseen branches under the two feet of snow. He continued on, branches whipping his face as he leapt over deadfalls. Expecting to hear gunshots, he slowed to a jog and then stopped behind a large pine tree, his breath nearly out of control.

He listened now. Nothing.

Then he saw it. A single light shone from where he had just come. The two of them had hesitated long enough to go back to the car for a flashlight, and now they were simply following his tracks. Who knew what else they had gotten at the car. Guns?

Standing idle, the cold caught up to him in a hurry, and he shook uncontrollably now. Move Jake. Move! He glanced about the forest. There was only one thing he could do. Back track to the road.

He ran off again, his arms trying to protect his face from branches. How far had he run? The road had to be soon, he thought, his feet and legs lifting high out of the snow with each step, trying his best to keep from gouging the souls of his bare feet again.

Shortly he saw an opening ahead, the swirling clouds offering a slight view of a meadow or field.

Coming to the edge of the opening, he hesitated among some smaller pines. If he entered, he knew he would be one big target, picked off like that airborne laser had dropped the Russian missile. Instead, he worked his way around the outside of the field.

There. The road. On the far end of the field, the road ran along the edge.

Out of breath and his extremities freezing, Jake stopped and glanced behind him. He couldn't see the light, and that wasn't particularly comforting.

He would have to run along the road for a hundred meters of open area, fully exposed to anyone to see, as he worked his way back toward the car. And then what? Could he reasonably expect them to have left the keys there?

Suddenly, from the same direction he planned to head, a car approached slowly down the frozen, snow-covered dirt road, its lights off. Jake ducked deep into the snow behind a pine tree.

He closed his eyes and his head ached. Held his breath and slowly let out some air.

Just as he thought the car would pass, it stopped, and Jake looked up to see the red tail lights brighten the car before going out.

Now he knew he was in trouble.

CHAPTER 4

Huddled in the deep snow, his legs numb, Jake heard a noise in the woods behind him. Slowly he glanced back and saw the light along the far edge of the meadow.

He was understandably confused. Had one stayed with the tracks while the other went for the car?

"Adams?" came a hushed voice from the car, an older Russian Volga sedan.

Jake shifted his head around. That wasn't the voice of the man or woman.

"Adams," came the voice again. "You wanna live, get your ass in here. I'm American."

He had no choice. His confusion would have to give way to survival and trust-the last of which was in short supply in his mind at the moment.

The driver's door opened, illuminating a man waving his arm to him.

Without further coaxing, Jake sprinted from the snow to the road and around to the front passenger seat.

Swinging the door open, he quickly assessed the driver, a man in his early forties, clean-cut and wearing a dark green parka.

"Get in, Jake! Let's go."

He did just that. The car pulled away as soon as he closed the door. Jake peered back behind him, and in the distance he saw two figures appear on the road with the light.

Jake looked at the driver more carefully now. "Who the hell are you?"

"The guy who just saved your ass." The driver turned up the heat and switched the fan to high.

"Thanks. But you didn't answer my question."

Sitting on the seat next to the man was a high-end set of night vision goggles. So Jake reasoned the guy had been slowly driving down the road with the goggles on, watching for any movement.

"Network," Jake said. "Who sent you?"

The guy laughed. "Toni said you could be a brusque son-of-a-bitch."

That was twice in the evening someone had mentioned his former girlfriend.

"Toni who?"

The guy shook his head. "This a test?" His eyes shifted toward Jake as he said, "Toni Contardo. Until six months ago, your live-in squeeze. Black hair that flows over strong shoulders, followed a bit lower by the nicest set of tits I'll never see. A New York Italian."

"Those two back there knew that much," Jake said. "You'll have to do better than that."

Reaching inside his coat, the man started to pull something out, but Jake grabbed his hand before he could pull it out.

"Let me help you with that," Jake said, as he put his hand inside the guy's coat and pulled out what the man had been reaching to retrieve. It was a passport. A dark burgundy U.S. passport. Jake flipped it to the back and found what he was looking for, an annotation that indicated this man had diplomatic immunity. Definitely a spook. Then he opened the passport to the front. It was official. Lance Turner. Born in Memphis, Tennessee.

The car came to the end of the road. The driver turned left toward Khabarovsk.

"All right?"

"Lance? Your parents must have wanted you to get your ass whipped in school."

"Ha. Ha. Gimme that." He took the passport from Jake and put it back in his pocket.

"So, you're a Network spook. How do I know you know Toni?"

"Because she's probably the most gorgeous officer we have." He hesitated and then said, "You two worked together in Italy years ago. Then, when you went private, you worked another case there with a Naval officer from a carrier. You took a bullet to the left temple on that carrier, and the hair still doesn't grow right there, from what I understand. You also had a little run-in with some Hungarians at her apartment, where you killed one and wounded another. Should I go on?"

His head ached even more thinking about that grazing shot he had taken in Italy. "That won't be necessary. How is Toni?"

The man's eyes shifted to the side as he gripped the steering wheel with both hands. "We haven't heard from her."

When Toni had left him in Austria, she had done so with great hesitation, knowing she would be working undercover in the Middle East. Her Italian looks could have passed for Arab with a little work, and her language skills were impeccable.

"Understand," Jake said. "What I don't understand, though, is how you found me."

The car started to reach the outskirts of Khabarovsk, but the traffic was nearly non-existent at that early hour.

"When you told the Network you were asked to observe the launch, I was sent from our consulate in Vladivostok to keep an eye on you. We had rumblings about a possible disruption from a few other countries in the area."

"Like?"

"I'm not—"

"At liberty. I know, but I just had an encounter with a few pissed-off Chinese."

Turner thought for a moment. "You sure they weren't North Korean?"

"It was dark. Could have been. I got a pretty good look at the woman, though."

That revelation made Turner twist his head toward Jake and then slowly turn back to the road. "Woman?"

"Yeah, and movie-star gorgeous."

"Shit!"

"What?"

"Can't be sure. I saw the two of them head into your hotel. But, like you said, it was dark. She looked familiar from a distance. If it was the agent we've been briefed on, you're lucky to be alive."

"Thanks for the confidence boost."

"No offense, but you have been out of the game for a while."

"Any reason they wanted to pick me up?"

"What'd they say?"

Jake shrugged. "Just wanted to know about the missile launch."

"That's it?"

"I left in a hurry. They might have wanted to know about the gross national product of Finland."

"Okay, but they probably know that's a hundred and thirty billion."

Jake stared at the guy.

"Economics major."

"Ah. So, back to the two Chinese who interrupted my sleep. You just let them take me?"

The Network officer thought for a long while as he stopped the car at a red light on the outskirts of the city. As he pulled away, he said, "I called it in. They wanted me to hold back. See what they wanted with you."

"And if they had killed me?"

"They didn't. And we had no reason to think they would. Besides, I was right behind you all the way."

"I didn't know that."

"True. Anyway, they wanted to know about the missile. What'd you tell them."

"The truth."

"What?"

"That the missile malfunctioned. What else is there?"

"Right."

This was not going well. The Network officer was giving him nothing. "Listen. If you want my help, you better start telling the truth."

Turner lifted his hands from the steering wheel. "What?"

"Like how the U.S. shot the missile down with its new Airborne Laser."

The officer's face twisted somewhat, and Turner tried to recover before he said, "Who told you that?"

Not exactly a denial. "Colonel Pushkina."

"Shit!"

"You think the government would keep it from him?"

"That's not it. Pushkina is missing."

"Taken like me?"

"Don't know."

Without saying another word, Turner pulled out his cell phone and punched in a number. He waited and then said, "Boone, One Seven Three Four." Listening for a few seconds, Turner finally said, "Got him here."

Two minutes passed as they traveled along the road that finally became familiar to Jake. They stopped and pulled over to the curb a half a block down from the Shevchenko Hotel.

Turner said into his phone, "Yes, sir," and then he flipped the phone shut and returned it to his jacket pocket.

"Well?"

"I was told to get you out of Russia."

"Just like that."

"Just like that," Turner repeated. "We're only twenty-five kilometers from China."

"China? Why the hell would I go there?"

Turner, more serious than ever, said, "Because your country needs you."

Jake had heard that before more than he would have liked to admit. How the hell had it come to this? Fly to Russia, Yuri had said. Watch the missile and drink some vodka. B.S. about the old days. Great. Now they were asking him to go to China. Just like the Air Force and the old CIA, this was obviously government voluntary. Do it or something nefarious will happen. It was always something, Jake knew.

♦

Huddled in the Volkswagen Santana, the heater working overtime, Li felt the cold reality of failure for the first time in years. Part of her wanted to rush back to Khabarovsk, find that bastard American, and the person who had picked him up on the road half naked, and do to him like she did to the man in San Francisco two months ago. The other part of her, the part that had been sexually excited by his skill at escaping, wanted to do things to him that was illegal in most countries.

Laughing Dragon put the car in gear and pulled away into the night. He pushed a tape into the player on the dash and The Beatles "The Fool on the Hill" broke the silence.

"That me," he said. "Just a Fool on the Hill." He laughed uncontrollably.

When he was done, she thought about their instructions, wondering if they could continue. "We have failed," she said softly, her eyes diverting toward the few stars she could see as the clouds parted.

He reached across her to the glove box and pulled out a silenced automatic pistol. Pointing it at her head, he said, "Then I shoot you. Send you to Hell."

She closed her eyes. Part of her wanted him to pull the trigger. She heard the hammer click back. Then her family would be free. They would no longer have this man and others hanging over them, waiting for failure like this, waiting for leverage to force her to do what she knew in her mind had to be done.

The hammer clicked loudly.

Opening her eyes, she turned to see the barrel a few inches from her face. "You sick bastard."

He lowered the gun and giggled like a little girl. "You get like me you play this game long enough."

Maybe so, she thought. Maybe she was already there and didn't know it. "We failed," she said again.

"No, no, no," Laughing Dragon said. "Everything happen for reason."

She was confused. "We didn't get the information from Adams. We should have killed him."

The car came to a stop at the end of the frozen road, and the driver paused there for a moment.

He shook his head as he said, "You don't know everything, Li. That always on purpose. In case you get caught."

"Are you saying we didn't need anything from Jake Adams?"

He smiled. "I bet he pissed off now." He hesitated, as if trying to search his brain to see how much he could tell her. "We know what happen to missile. American laser shoot it down."

With that revelation, her brows rose. "The laser from San Francisco?"

"That's why you go there now," he said. "We need the software."

She thought about the man she was running there. How she wasn't sure if he would deliver. Glancing at the gun, she knew what she had to do. The laser worked. "I understand," she finally said.

"Good. Now, about that Beatles album. You find first edition Abby Road, perfect condition. . . I'm very happy."

He cackled as he turned the car left toward Khabarovsk and slowly pulled out onto the roughly paved road.

CHAPTER 5

Eareckson Air Station
Shemya, Alaska

Wind whipped across the frozen Earth and stirred up clouds of snow on the remote island at the western edge of the Aleutian Islands. Visibility at the nearby airport was at zero, which matched the temperature before the wind chill. Adding the thirty mile an hour gusts, it felt like closer to thirty below zero.

Eareckson had been Shemya Air Base until a few years ago, first inhabited by the U.S. military in 1943 after kicking the Japanese off the island, and continuously since then with a peak of some 1,500 personnel in the 1970s. Now there were only 85 people on the two-mile by four-mile rock; mostly government contractors there to help with re-fueling military aircraft on the long flights from stateside bases to Asia. But that would soon change.

Standing outside a brick building built in the mid-80s, trying desperately to keep his cigar lit, was the future commander, Colonel Tim Powers. In the old days, the colonel could have simply lit up in his office and enjoyed this vice without losing an appendage to frostbite. Now, though, because of Air Force-wide regulations, the little pleasure he got from the cigar was hardly worth the effort.

Only hours ago they had landed in their modified Boeing 747, which now sat huddled comfortably in a hardened hangar, technicians combing over the craft and ensuring all was well with the advanced Airborne Laser, with its high-energy Chemical Oxygen Iodine Laser (COIL) system.

The door opened and a man in a parka approached the colonel.

"Sir, nothing's going in or out of the airport for at least the next twelve hours." The voice was Senior Master Sergeant Gary Isham, the future squadron's first sergeant. Future, because the squadron would not be completely manned and operational for another six months.

"Thanks, Gary. I had a feeling. The pilot said we were lucky to land."

"What'll the fallout be from your shot?"

The colonel thought about that. He had been placed in charge of converting this old air base, used during the Cold War to pick up a first strike by the Soviets by both ICBM missiles and Sub-launched Ballistic Missiles, into a sophisticated testing facility for the new airborne laser interceptor technology. The older Cobra Dane phased array radar had served well to track and collect data on Soviet and Russian test launches to the Kamchatka impact area and the broader impact area of the northern Pacific Ocean in compliance with the START, START II and INF treaties. The radar had variously been used by NORAD, Air Force Space Command and the Air Intelligence Agency. But now, still under construction, was the follow-on to Cobra Dane, which would track missile launches and relay that information to laser sites in central Alaska, which would then shoot down any missile fired from Russia, China, or, more likely, North Korea.

In the past six months, Colonel Powers had been in charge of construction of this new radar, and, as far as the U.S. was concerned, their mission had gone unnoticed, he was sure. In fact, he was equally sure that the Russians had no idea they had re-opened this facility. From any satellite shot, the base looked deserted.

"The politicians can worry about that shit," the colonel said, sucking on his cigar and bringing it to a glowing orange.

"You got another one of those, Sir?"

"Jane doesn't want you smokin' these nasty things," the commander said. He smiled at his first sergeant, and then said, "Screw her if she can't take a joke." He reached inside his coat and pulled out another cigar, handing it to the sergeant.

"You took the words outta my mouth, Sir." He accepted the cigar and then lit it from the commander's, drawing in as hard as he could to keep it lit.

The commander had come to depend on his first sergeant ever since they were first stationed together in Germany years ago. They had both returned to the States around the same time, picking up assignments with Space Command in Colorado Springs. Six months ago, Colonel Powers had requested Senior Master Sergeant Isham by name to help lead his troops in Alaska. In fact, almost everyone in the unit had worked with the colonel at some point in their career. The mission was so important he only wanted those he knew for this assignment. If the colonel didn't know them personally, then the first sergeant had known them at some time in his career.

"Sounds like the old software worked as advertised, Sir. Why the need for new software?"

The colonel raised his head and let out a stream of smoke. "They're always upgrading, Gary. We had the advantage with this first strike. We knew when they would launch, where they would launch from, and the trajectory was predictable. The new software will help with the land-based system while the missiles are out over the arctic and are on a less predictable flight pattern. We're talkin' about concentrating a beam of light the width of a Dodge on an object flying at over twenty-five thousand kilometers per hour."

"Damn."

"Damn right," the colonel said. "That's one helluva project in vector calculus and physics."

"We gonna make our operational deadline, Colonel?"

Failure was a prospect the colonel couldn't fathom. He had never failed at anything in his life, and this would be no exception.

"The Russians now know we can shoot down their missiles, Gary. They gotta be shitin' their pants right about now."

They both sucked on their cigars in unison.

The colonel only wished his group was as far along as everyone thought.

CHAPTER 6

Palo Alto, California

Fog shrouded the entire Bay Area, despite the fact that it was early afternoon. Soon rush hour traffic would clog California 101 to a near standstill.

Clifford Johansen sat at his desk on the third floor of the Brightstar International industrial complex. He looked out at the parking lot, spotted his ten year old Toyota Camry sitting in a sea of BMWs and Mercedes, and knew that what he was about to do was the right thing. It had to be.

He swiveled his slight frame around in his chair, shifting his black-framed glasses askew on his narrow nose. With his middle finger he shoved the glasses back into place-a reaction that had almost gotten him beat up in high school. He laughed to himself thinking about how many people he had, supposedly through an inadvertent reaction, flipped off over the years. His clueless colleagues at Brightstar never seemed to get the point.

Rising above the cubicle wall and seeing the normal afternoon shuffle of workers trying to appear busy, Cliff turned to his computer, clicked through security, and found the files he had hidden days before. He had marked them with innocuous file names that would not catch anyone's eye, and then compressed and zipped them. He should have saved them to a DVD, but he could be checked at the security post on his departure. As he knew with all computers and with all software, there was always another way. Always a way to make things work.

"Cliff, what's up?"

Cliff nearly jumped from his chair as he hit a key to change his monitor to a mountain scene screen saver.

The voice was from one of his office friends, Steve Lempi. His office friend because, although they talked often at work, they never did anything together after they left the Brightstar compound at the end of the day. Part of that was distance. Steve lived in Redwood City, while he lived across the Bay in Fremont. The other part, Cliff was sure, was that Steve was not a typical computer geek. With his perfect blond hair, his athletic physique, and his charming personality, he had a better chance than most at Brightstar of actually having a life outside this compound.

"Steve, never sneak up on a programmer like that," Cliff said, shifting his glasses up on his nose. "I could have lost an entire day of code." This wasn't true and Steve knew it, but since they were both programmers, each understood the severity of losing anything dealing with one of their projects.

Steve leaned against the cubicle wall, the sweat stains visible under his left arm and his biceps nearly bursting out the white cotton shirt. "Back it up and make a copy." That was the mantra of Brightstar.

"Right," Cliff said. "That's why our drives are always maxed out." Not true. They had enough storage capacity to run a small, third world country. Like France.

Steve had a look on his broad face like he had something important on his mind, but he wasn't sure how to ask the question. Finally, he stooped down low, looked around behind him, and whispered, "Aren't you working the ABL project?"

Cliff stood up and peered over his cubicle at the spaces on either side. They were both empty. Then he sat and turned to Steve. "Even if I was, I couldn't tell you."

Steve smiled. "I'll take that as a yes."

"No—"

"Don't worry. I'm not gonna tell anyone."

The ABL project was a government contract for Airborne Lasers that Cliff had worked on for the past two years. It was highly compartmentalized among various government agencies, the Air Force, and at least three private corporations-with Brightstar the lead contractor. The system was in place for major testing of their new software in the next few weeks.

"What do you want from me, Steve?"

"Nothing. Just making conversation." He hesitated and glanced behind him. "A bunch of Group Five are going out for drinks after work tonight.

Down at the Hard Drive Bar. Thought you might like to join us. Five o'clock."

Group Five was Steve's team; his was Group Seven. They usually didn't mix for fear of slipping up and mentioning their current projects.

"Better not," Cliff said. "I have a date tonight."

Steve look surprised. "With a girl?"

"No, a dog. What the hell do ya think?"

"Damn. Communications needs to put out a press release. Programmer gets date."

"Bite me!"

"Is that B.Y.T.E.?"

Cliff stared at his friend for a moment, and then said, "Thanks for the invite."

Steve took that as his cue to leave. "Bring her by. Group Five is a wild bunch."

Cliff nodded and waved as his friend left. Then he stood up to make sure he was really gone, and spotted him making his way toward the restroom.

He took a deep breath and noticed his hands shaking. He shook his hands until they settled down. Then he went back to his computer, found the files, and stopped. Could he do this? He sighed and clicked away at his computer. First he bypassed the firewall software to make sure he could send without being interrupted. Then he entered the router and disabled the physical firewall.

Now he had thirty seconds.

He clicked the keyboard furiously, sending the files. But, even zipped, they were large and needed time.

Twenty seconds.

The physical firewall would automatically reset after thirty seconds and could alert security that files were leaving the internal system.

Fifteen seconds.

And there was still forty percent to send.

Come on, come on.

Ten seconds.

Lag. Damn it! Thirty percent left.

Five...four...three.

The Files Sent message came up, and Cliff quickly worked his way out, enabling the software firewall as he got out. That was too close, he thought. Now his whole body was shaking and sweat streaked his forehead. Damn. He clicked into his registry and found the record of his sending the files. He deleted that and the backup. That was too close. Maybe Steve's little reminder had saved his ass this time. "Back it up and make a copy." The Brightstar system was programmed to do just that, even if the users forgot.

He checked his watch. It was almost time to quit for the day. He had to compose himself. He wiped his forehead with a tissue and breathed in deep, just like Li had told him. Settled, he shut down his computer and gathered his jacket from a corner stand. Now he just had to stay calm long enough to get through security.

♦

At home in Fremont, Cliff got onto his computer. He quickly accessed the files he had sent, and, satisfied that they would be safe in their new home, he got off the computer and went to his refrigerator for a beer. He shook his head at the contents of his refrigerator. There was a six pack of a microbrew from Bend, Oregon, and that was ironic. His old college friend from the University of Oregon had sent him the beer from his hometown. Cliff had gone there skiing two months ago, just before Christmas, and had set up a server in the man's house in the quiet subdivision along the Deschutes River. His friend had no idea that Cliff had just sent him some of the most classified programming in the world. Programs that would control the firing system of the Airborne Laser, and eventually the entire land-based laser system. But he had sent more than just programming. More than just the project that he was working on. He had sent schematics of the entire Airborne Laser project. Files that were supposed to be compartmentalized. But fear of loss had worked in his favor. Brightstar had been so worried about losing data to computer failure, that they had opened themselves up for a loss far more damaging. That is, if he went through with it.

He checked his watch. He had just forty-five minutes to meet Li at her house in Union City. His heart raced just thinking about their meeting.

He hurried from his house and drove off in his Camry.

Just as she informed him, he took a different route to her place, doubling back and constantly checking his rear view mirror for a tail. It was all so cloak and dagger, considering he had really done nothing wrong to this point. Nothing had transferred hands.

As he got closer to her house, excitement entered his body. He wanted to be with her again. Needed to be with her again.

He parked down the block a ways in front of a house for sale. The neighbors would think he was checking out the new house. Nothing more. No reason to call the cops for a strange car parking there.

He got to Li's house and she opened the door for him. She was so beautiful. Her long dark hair flowed straight to the top of broad shoulders. Although she told him her family was originally from Hong Kong, her eyes seemed more Mongolian to him. At least according to the Discovery Channel special he had watched a few years ago.

"You're two minutes late," Li said. Then she smiled and kissed him before retreating toward the living room.

He watched her perfect, slim body move across the room and settle into the leather sofa. She was wearing loose silk pants, and, even though they were black, he could tell through the back lighting that she wasn't wearing anything under them. On top she wore a Stanford sweat shirt with the sleeves pushed up to the elbows.

The stereo played Bach lightly in the background. Cliff took a seat on the sofa next to her. He wanted her so badly, but he knew not to push the issue. She would want answers first.

"How is your mother?" Cliff asked her. She had gone back to China for a while when she had found out her mother was sick.

"She's better."

"Glad to hear that."

She narrowed her eyes toward him. "How close are you?" she asked.

He didn't want any of this to end. "Very close." He ran his hand along her thigh.

She stopped him, grabbing his hand. "How close?"

He thought for a moment. "What about the money?"

"You give me the files, I give you the money."

"You give me the money, I give you the files."

"So, you have them?"

Damn. He had to think fast now. "I have access to them. I've...found a way."

She took her hand from his and ran it across the erection that had grown in his pants. "I need the files tonight. You transfer the files and I'll transfer the money."

It was a never-ending cycle. How could he get the money before he gave her the files? Then just last night he had come up with a way, which is why he had transferred the files today. He explained the plan to her. When he was done, she simply smiled and nodded agreement. Then she unzipped his pants and took him in her mouth.

CHAPTER 7

Beijing, China

Jake walked calmly along the stone sidewalk in a back street two blocks from Tiananmen Square, the darkness broken only by distant street lights and the occasional lantern marking a bar or cafe. Although it was closing in on midnight, the streets were still full of life. Not like Paris or London or New York. But his native Portland would be nearly deserted at that time of night on a Wednesday.

Accustomed to working at night, Jake's eyes adjusted well to the darkness, and his other senses would heighten along with them, he knew. Time couldn't dull training and experience.

It was at times like this, when he had no idea why he was here at this hour, that he wished he had his normal 9mm automatic strapped under his left arm. Just in case. But, unlike Europe, he had no contacts in China who could acquire such weapons. Nor did he think, until now, that he would need one. After all, his back story indicated he was only in Beijing to accompany an American businessman, who had just that morning signed a huge fiber optics deal that would link hard lines and speedy data transfer to not only every corner of the city, but also, he hoped, to every major city in China. Jake had learned as much as he could about the man in the last few hours in case anyone cared to ask the question.

But now Jake was on his own. He had followed the American to the airport earlier in the day and then gone back to his hotel in the Qianmen region, just six blocks from his current location. And then, as he rested in his room trying to figure out what the Network had in store for him in the next few days before flying back to Austria, he had gotten the strange phone call. That was five hours ago. The caller, a man of indistinguishable age or ethnicity, although Jake was sure he must have been Western, had simply said to meet him behind the Museum to Chinese History if he wanted to find out about his old girlfriend, Toni Contardo. It was a ruse, he knew.

He hadn't heard from Toni in six months. They had been living together in a nice apartment overlooking the river in Innsbruck, he thinking their relative domestication was actually working out, and she obviously thinking the tranquility of seclusion in Austria reason enough to go back to work for the Network. So, as far as he knew, she had done just that, having first gone through extensive Arabic language training before being assigned to...well, that was the problem. He had no idea where she was.

So the caller would know that, he had said. Then he either had a choice to hit the sack early and take a tour of the Great Wall in the morning, or end up in a dark alley at midnight to meet someone he didn't know for unknown reasons. Jake didn't think for a moment that he would find out anything about Toni. But, hope was like the concept of happiness. You never knew you had found it until after it had passed.

He turned from the relatively busy sidewalk down a narrow lane, where only a lone woman shot her eyes away from him and scurried in the opposite direction. After making it halfway down the street, Jake stopped and leaned against a wall in the shadows, glancing across the narrow street at a back gate to the museum.

On both ends of the street was a clamor of voices and footsteps and laughter, but here the street had cleared and he was alone.

His eyes shifted back and forth with each sound.

Suddenly, out of the shadows of the courtyard across the street, behind the gates, there was movement. Then Jake heard the lighter flicker and watched the glow of a cigarette being lit.

That was his sign.

He crossed the alley and opened the gate with a slight squeak, slid inside, and moved toward the glowing cigarette.

"That's close enough," came a muffled voice from the shadows. It was almost a whisper. "To your left, into the darkness."

The cigarette dropped to the ground and the man twisted his foot over it as Jake moved into the shadows.

"You could have just come to my hotel," Jake said. "We could be drinking a beer right now instead of freezing our asses off out in the darkness."

Jake was close enough to hear air forcing its way out of the man's nostrils, so he knew it was the same guy who had called him earlier.

"Asthma," Jake said.

"What?"

"You have asthma, so the Network sends you to Beijing in February with all this Gobi sand in the air. How smart is that?"

The man gave a slight laugh. "I heard you were a smart ass."

Jake flicked on a penlight, illuminating the man's face for a second, and quickly turned it off.

"What the hell are you doing?" The man whispered loudly.

"I like to see who I'm dealing with. Show me some I.D."

"Are you on drugs?"

"I must be," Jake said, "or I wouldn't be standing in a dark alley at midnight with an asthmatic Network man who wants to use me for some reason."

The man laughed again through his nose. It was barely audible, but Jake was comforted somewhat knowing the Network had actually hired someone with a sense of humor.

"What do you want from me?" Jake asked.

There was silence, so Jake started to walk away.

"Wait."

A hand grasped his arm, and Jake removed it, twisted the man's arm around, and jammed the guy's face into the metal fence. With Jake's free hand, he clasped his fingers around the left side of his face and placed his thumb behind the guy's left ear, applying pressure. Most people could last only a few seconds without feeling like their brains would pop out of their ears. This Network guy made it a full thirty seconds. Impressive.

"All right!" he forced out through his teeth. "Inside right pocket."

Jake slid his left hand from his grasp and inside the guy's front pocket, retrieving a passport. He still had a hold of the guy with a right arm twist, but now he needed his light, and that would take two hands.

He took two steps back and let go of the arm. Jake could hear the man rotating his right arm back into place as he pulled the light from his pocket and shone it on the passport, cupped inside his jacket. It was a standard U.S. diplomatic passport. Definitely Network. He turned off the light and slapped the passport against the guy's chest.

"Okay, Mr. Brian Armstrong...what do you want from me?"

"I need you," he said. "I heard what you did in Odessa years ago."

Jake hadn't thought about Odessa for a long time. So much had gone right, but so much had also gone tragically wrong there. Then it all clicked. The face had looked familiar. And now the name.

"Any relation to Quinn Armstrong?"

The man hesitated. "Quinn was my brother."

Damn! "I'm sorry."

"He died for his country."

Still, Jake might have been able to save the man's life. They had worked together in Odessa, and Quinn had been killed by his own boss, a rogue Network station chief.

"I'm sorry," Jake repeated.

"I read the report," Armstrong said. "You had no idea my little brother would be killed. And you did bring down the guy who shot him."

Bring down was not really true. Jake had found out about the corrupt officer and was present when he ate his own gun.

Changing the subject, Jake said, "So why me?"

"Easy. You were with the Network. I can trust you. And...."

"And nobody knows me in China."

"Right."

"What do you need?" Jake asked.

"Meet me tomorrow morning at ten in the center of Tiananmen Square."

He didn't hear the sound first, but Jake did see the flash. He grabbed Armstrong by the coat and pulled him to the ground. Now the clinking of metal against metal followed each flash as bullets glanced off the gate and ricocheted into the night.

Instinctively, Jake went for his gun, which wasn't there.

CHAPTER 8

They ran. Then they split up and ran some more. Finding himself in unfamiliar city streets, Jake finally found a cab and told the driver to take him to the China Theatre on the western edge of Beijing near the zoo.

As the cab drove off, Jake checked behind them. Nothing. Maybe the shooter had followed Armstrong.

When the cab reached the China Theatre, Jake paid the cab driver and then located the bus stop across the street. He spent the next hour transferring from bus to bus on his way back to his hotel.

Jake spent the rest of the night holed up in his hotel trying to figure out how he had gotten himself into another mess like this. Trouble seemed to follow him around, as if someone had placed a GPS tracking device at the base of his skull.

♦

The Network officer, Brian Armstrong, had said to meet him at ten the next morning in the center of Tiananmen Square. Jake was now, ten minutes past the hour, standing against a far edge watching the most likely entrance to the expansive square, the side directly across the street from the Gate of Heavenly Peace with the ten-foot photo of Chairman Mao looming down on visitors. At this hour, the large tour groups moved about the stone surface like schools of fish. Food vendors with little carts hoped to attract the early lunch crowd, while others wandered about trying to hawk packs of postcards under the watchful eyes of barely-pubescent underfed soldiers in green uniforms. Jake guessed the place was a zoo in

July, but the tourist season in China's February was limited.

Glancing up at posts strategically located about the square, Jake noticed cameras swiveling about on top of each. Then a small truck moved slowly about the large stone surface, with cameras also working overtime. There would be no repeat of 1989, Jake thought. He imagined the blood from that massacre still settled among the mortar.

With all of the activity, it was possible for the Network man to slip in without Jake's knowledge. And, considering he had only seen the man for a brief moment prior to the bullets flying and their departure in different directions, Jake wasn't a hundred percent sure if he could pick him out in the large mass of humanity. The only advantage he had was the fact that most of the American tourists were in groups, and Armstrong was a six foot, blond Anglo among a sea of shorter Asians.

Finally, Jake saw the man step out of a bus at the Tiananmen Gate and hurry across the large expanse to where the center could be located. There was no actual center or obvious center. When Armstrong got to a point in the square, he looked straight ahead for a moment before slowly swiveling his head and eyes in each direction. He couldn't have been more obvious.

Jake shook his head and started toward the man. He had wanted to wait for a while to see if Armstrong had been followed. He had to think that nearly every employee of the U.S. government working out of the embassy had at least one shadow. Yet, in this situation, Jake felt it best to simply move forward and see what the man had on his mind.

Something wasn't right, Jake could tell. But he stepped forward and pulled out a large map of Beijing just before he reached Armstrong.

"Do you know where in the hell I can find someone with brains?" Jake asked the man, pointing to a place on his map.

"You're a funny bastard, you know that?" Armstrong pointed to a place on the map. "Over my left shoulder, about fifty yards back, you'll see a man with a camera. That's Number One Son. One of three tails I get every day. That's why I need you." He smiled and pointed toward the Forbidden City.

"So then why did you bring me here to be photographed?" Jake said, marking another point on the map with his finger. "There are more cameras in this square than all of Hollywood."

"Because they wouldn't expect a contact here for that very reason. Listen, we can't do this for long. I need your help. Go to Murphy's on

Qianmen at noon. It's an Irish pub. You'll meet a big guy there with red hair. Name is Steve Anderson." Now he turned and pointed toward the Gate of Heavenly Peace, just one tourist helping another.

"Gee, how likely is it I'll find a red-headed expat at an Irish pub?" Jake said softly, nodding his head and pointing off to nowhere.

"Noon," Armstrong repeated.

Jake started to walk off.

"The map was a nice touch," the Network man said.

Jake smiled. "Well, somebody has to do the thinking around here," he said over his shoulder.

Walking slowly away, Jake wondered if he'd end up on some intelligence briefing. He continued over to the Gate of Heavenly Peace and looked it over for a moment, spending time to make sure Armstrong had cleared the square, and that his friend had gone with him. Then Jake took a long route back to his hotel, making damn sure he wasn't followed.

All of this scrutiny had him wondering again what was going on. What did they have planned for him?

After laying around his room for a short while, he started off toward the Irish pub. It would take him at least forty-five minutes to go the six blocks from his hotel to the pub, making sure he was not followed.

For a Thursday lunch time, the pub was fairly quiet. Jake guessed they did a better business at night, especially on the weekends. He took a seat at the end of the bar with a wide view of the entire place, and ordered a Guinness. Two minutes later, a huge man roamed through the front door and took a seat in a booth at the far end of the main room. Even with the relative darkness of the bar, Jake guessed this guy could light the booth with his orange head.

When Jake was sure the guy was alone, he picked up his beer and walked over to the large guy with the neon locks.

"Steve?" Jake asked.

The guy nodded his head for Jake to sit down.

Jake took a seat. "Let's see some I.D."

The large man looked confused.

"It was a simple request," Jake assured him.

"I've heard you're an obstinate bastard," the man said.

"Before we start calling each other names, let's make sure we know the real ones."

The man shook his thick red head and then produced a blue U.S. passport. Jake took a quick look and handed it back. "Now the wallet."

"What?"

Jake shrugged. "So, you're Steve Anderson. That doesn't tell me shit."

Reluctantly, the man pulled out his wallet and handed it across the table. Jake scanned the contents and handed it back.

"Satisfied?" Anderson asked.

"Depends on what you want from me."

A Chinese waitress came around and asked them if they would like to order lunch. Anderson ordered a Guinness and said they'd need a few minutes.

"We..."

"Just a minute. Who is we?" Jake looked around the room.

"I represent a group in Washington."

"The name!"

"The Western Institute." He barely whispered the words.

"The conservative think tank?"

Jake had guessed for years that there was more to those think tanks, liberal or conservative, than was released in the charter or mission statements.

Anderson ignored his comments. "We need your help."

"There was something about information about a certain friend of mine. Where she might be at this time."

"I don't know that," Anderson said. "You'll have to discuss that with Arm...your other contact."

This guy was a genius. Probably Mensa quality. But, realistically, Jake didn't expect to get any real information out of him about Toni.

"What do you want? And why me?"

Before he could answer, the waitress brought him his beer. They both ordered the lamb soup and bread and the woman took off.

"You come highly recommended," he said.

"I guessed that. Otherwise you would have asked to see my I.D. But you had already seen my face in a briefing at the embassy."

Anderson seemed to blush. "Your record with the Network is impressive, along with your work in Air Force Intelligence before that. I was particularly inspired by your work in Kurdistan."

Work that had nearly gotten Jake killed, and had almost allowed a large group of terrorists to produce the most deadly biological weapon ever conceived. Not to mention the loss of two Network officers in Odessa, including Armstrong's brother.

"You have something like that in mind for me?" Jake asked. "Before you answer, remember I was almost killed, and that we lost some good officers on that mission."

"I know. And you also caught a rogue officer."

Jake shook his head. "I'm not about to stick my nose in Network business. If they've got a problem, which I won't doubt for a minute, they can handle it themselves."

"Would you let me explain?" he said. "I'm part of the Jake Adams fan club. The Institute is well aware of your work. But China is different. When your old comrade Yuri Pushkina asked you to observe the missile launch, that got us thinking."

"Great. Glad someone's thinking." Something switched in Jake's mind, and he shook his head ever so slightly as he said, "You bastards knew we'd shoot down that missile."

"That had to happen. The fact that you were there was irrelevant."

Jake leaned across the table. "What about the fact that I almost got my ass killed?"

Anderson hesitated. "I'm sorry about that, but that's why we needed you in China."

Jake was about to dress him down with regard to his ancestry, when the waitress brought them their soup.

Once the woman left, Jake said, "So I'm here in China. What made you think I'd pop to attention like a good little soldier?"

"Toni is here and she needs your help."

Jake had been sipping his soup and nearly choked.

"What? She's supposed to be in the Middle East."

"She was...but now she's needed here."

"You're fulla shit."

Anderson took a large spoonful of soup and then wiped his lip with his napkin. "Maybe. But in this case, I'm telling you the truth."

"Why would she need my help?"

"I've been trying to tell you, China is different. The visa requirements are so restrictive, they can control who comes and goes much more thoroughly than the European countries. Here they know everyone. They don't know you. We got you here on a legitimate tourist visa. You entered from Russia after leaving Austria; not the U.S. You can travel on that visa. You should have enough time."

"Time for what?"

Anderson hesitated, glancing about the room. "We need you in Manchuria."

"Would you cut with the cryptic shit and tell me what you need."

He leaned across the table toward Jake. "The Chinese have built a facility in Manchuria to test lasers. Technology we believe they stole under the last administration's watch."

"And I take it this isn't for surgery. You're talking about laser weapons. Just like the one we used to shoot down the Russian missile."

"Right." He hesitated only long enough to scoop a spoonful of cooling soup down his throat. "We just need you to go up and take a look at their facility."

"I'm sure you have all the satellite photos you need." Jake thought about it for a second. Nothing made sense. This guy wasn't telling him everything. "Look. This sounds like a fool's errand."

"The photos you talk about...that's how we initially found out about this. We caught them transporting an item that looked too familiar. But everything is covered now. They've built a helluva facility there."

"You're trying to get my ass killed," Jake said. "I get within twenty miles of that joint and they'll string me up by my nuts."

The red-haired consultant laughed and pointed his spoon at Jake. "You're funny." He shifted his eyes at the front door and then back toward Jake. "Under the table there's a briefcase with all the info you'll need. There's also a digital camera with a cell phone attachment. You shoot the photos and transmit them immediately to the first number programmed on the phone."

"I don't like this."

"You'll be doing a great service for your country."

"I've done enough for my country."

Anderson glared at Jake. "You can never do too much."

"Then why don't you go?"

"Because, although I'm not known in China, one look and they track me to the Washington think tank. It wouldn't take much of a leap for them to assume I'm working for the government."

"Are you?"

He shot his eyes through Jake. "About as much as you are, but...also like you, I spent a good deal of my adult life in the military and other agencies. You gonna help us or not?"

"I'm not going to find Toni Contardo in Manchuria."

He shrugged. "They told me she was there. You don't guess they'd lie about something like that?" He smiled broadly.

Bastards. "How important is this technology?"

His expression turned grave as he leaned toward Jake. "If the Chinese have a laser missile defense, it will be a quantum leap in technology for them. They'd have no fear of missile attack from Taiwan, Russia, India or the U.S. Not to mention the North Koreans."

"And that's bad because...."

"Because it throws everything out of balance."

"You mean it puts them on par with the U.S."

"It makes them a second superpower with close to a billion and a half folks."

Jake had to admit that sounded somewhat scary, but the technology was defensive. And, if they had stolen that technology from America, that wasn't nice.

Anderson continued, "You haven't asked about the money."

Jake's eyes glanced down under the table.

"It'll be sent to your private account in Liechtenstein."

"You bastards." Only Toni was supposed to know about that account.

He smiled. "Have a nice trip."

Jake pulled the leather briefcase from under the table. Steve Anderson hadn't come in with it, so it must have been there all along waiting for their meeting.

Walking down the sidewalk toward his hotel, Jake wondered again what in the hell he was doing. Did he have a death wish? The first thing he would have to do was extract the programmed numbers from the cell phone and memorize them before deleting them from the internal memory. These guys had a lot to learn about undercover work.

CHAPTER 9

Washington, D.C.

The large dinner gathering included members of the senate, the house, white house staff, and business people from mostly high tech industries. It was the kind of function that would have been illegal if either side of the aisle didn't need the money and had actually taken a real vote on campaign finance reform. But this was business as usual in Washington.

Picking up a glass of Champaign from a waiter's tray, General Wayne Boles, U.S. Air Force retired, nodded and smiled at his target as he approached the White House Chief of Staff, Karl Oestreich. General Boles and Oestreich had worked together for two years under the secretary of defense during the former president's term. Oestreich had moved up nicely in the past few years, while Boles had bolted for the private sector and was now the director of The Western Institute, the conservative think tank.

"Wayne," the Chief of Staff said, "glad you could make it." He put his arm around the general and pulled him aside to one wall. "How are things?"

Boles smiled. "I assume you mean in China."

The Chief of Staff raised his brows in agreement.

"We hired Jake Adams to look into the matter."

Oestreich thought for a moment and sipped his wine. "That name sounds familiar."

"It should," Boles said. "When we were at Defense, he saved our collective asses in Kurdistan and the Ukraine."

"Right. Caught them with that biological agent and killed a rogue Network officer in Odessa."

"Well, I understand the officer killed himself, but, yeah, that's the guy."

"Wasn't he also the guy who caught the Hungarians and that German company ripping off some computer technology from the Joint Strike Fighter?"

"Yep!"

"Looks like you got the right guy."

General Boles glanced around the room, acknowledging a senator from Colorado with a nod. "I'm not sure about this."

"What. Why not?" The Chief of Staff moved closer, his voice a mere whisper. "The Chinese stole our laser technology. Don't forget that. And they did it while we were both at Defense. I don't think I need to remind you of that."

"Is the President aware of this?"

Oestreich's expression flashed from a fake smile to anger and then back to a smirk. "Does it matter?"

"It does to me," the general said.

"We have complete deniability on this," Oestreich assured him. "Adams gets caught and he has no tie to the administration. He's just a curious tourist."

"So, we hang him out to dry?"

"This is what he does for a living. He knows the score."

Boles grabbed the Chief of Staff on the forearm. "He was an Air Force officer who worked for me at one time."

Oestreich looked down at the general's hand, which slowly removed. "We'll do what we can behind the scenes, but push comes to shove and we deny any knowledge. You knew that going in." The Chief of Staff patted his old friend on the back and started to leave. "You better hope he's as good as you say he is." And now louder, Oestreich said, "You have a good time tonight, Wayne." He smiled and walked away.

The general was steaming inside, but he maintained his composure as he walked about the room with his empty glass. When a waiter came around now, the general put his glass down and picked up two in exchange.

Redding, California

"This friend of yours," Li said, peering sideways at Cliff Johansen from the front seat of her Isuzu Trooper. "Does he know we're coming?"

They had been driving from the Bay Area since dawn, picking up Interstate 5 in Sacramento, and would soon turn onto Highway 97 toward Oregon.

"He has no idea." Cliff was reading a technical manual on internet servers. "Like I said, though, we're old college friends."

"I think I should stay in a hotel," she said.

Cliff was thinking he would rather she come to his friend's house with him. She was gorgeous, and all through college neither of them had dated anyone close to her quality. In fact, they both could have counted their total dates on one hand.

He looked over at her. "It's only a couple of days."

"One night," she said emphatically. "You get what you need and we move on."

"Part of it," he corrected her. "We get part of it, you transfer the money, and then we go for the rest."

She shook her head. "We transfer part of the money."

"Well...right."

Cliff thought about his plan as he watched her drive down the road. He wanted to soak as much time as he could with her, for he knew that once she got what she wanted, and she had no more use for him, she was gone. That would be hard for him to take. God she was a hottie. He also knew that he would probably not ever return to Brightstar. Although he had called in sick while driving north, it would be nearly impossible for him to look those people in the eye again after what he had taken. He kept telling himself it was only data and pixels. But deep down he knew it was far worse than that. And his likelihood of being caught? Damn near zero. That brought a smile to his face. The old hacker in him.

♦

Two cars back on the freeway was a brown Ford Taurus driven by the man Cliff Johansen had come to know in the past six months as Steve Lempi, programmer for Brightstar's Group Five. A man who was actually special agent Drew Fisher with the Network's internal operations division.

Fisher checked his watch. Damn. He was late. Although he had already called in sick to Brightstar, he had not talked with his supervisor from Portland in two days.

He picked up his cell phone and punched in a number.

"Yeah, it's me. Our little rabbit's on the run." He hesitated long enough to pass a car, while still keeping one car between him and the Trooper.

"I don't know where he's going. We just passed through Redding heading north. He has friends in Eugene."

They were passing now through the Shasta Lake area. "Damn, this is pretty up here. Shasta Lake. Right, I remembered his friend in Bend. You think he's heading there?"

He drove across a high bridge and through a narrow mountain pass. "Right. I'll appreciate the help."

If they turned onto north Highway 97 at Weed, then he'd know they were going to Bend, Oregon. If they stayed on I-5, it would be Eugene. Either way, he had it covered.

CHAPTER 10

Shenyang, China

The night train from Beijing lumbered slowly into the Huanggutun Railway station on the western edge of the city, the sun still an hour or so from rising.

Jake Adams opened his eyes and shifted in his seat. He was in a compartment with seven other people, early in the evening speaking a language he didn't know, and eventually drifting off to sleep and speaking only the universal language of snores and heavy breathing. He had not slept much, though.

After his meeting with Steve Anderson, the think tank wonk, he had gone back to his hotel room and looked through the information. Most he had memorized and destroyed, and the rest he carried in a small backpack, which sat now at his feet.

He was to meet an agent in Shenyang, who would take him north to Harbin on the old Russian Manchurian Railroad. The next day they would travel to an undisclosed location in the northern frontier.

The train came to a halt and Jake waited for the others to leave before picking up his small backpack and slinging it over his shoulder. He glanced out the window, saw people waiting on a platform, bundled and their breath flowing in plumes of white, and realized he had only his lined leather jacket with him. Obviously not enough for this weather.

He wandered out and down the corridor, through the cheaper seats that would have made the airlines look lavish and comfortable, and then exited toward the main train station.

Immediately, cold air rushed toward him, as if he were in a wind tunnel. He quickened his pace.

Once inside the main building, he shifted his eyes at the high ceilings, and then made his way through a sea of people toward the train schedule board that took up nearly one entire wall. He was to stand there viewing the schedule until his contact approached him with the pre-determined signal. He hated this, not knowing the name of his contact or what he'd look like. Only the discussion would reveal the true contact. And that bothered him. He could be standing there like an idiot for hours.

"Harbin is nice this time of year," came a soft voice from behind. Nearly perfect English. But something unexpected.

He hesitated to turn around. "Isn't it a little cold this time of year. I heard it was like Siberia."

"Mr. Adams," the voice said. "We must go. Our train leaves in ten minutes."

He turned now to view a young woman of perhaps twenty-five. She was nearly five-six, with the most stunning facial features he had seen since his arrival in China. She embraced him firmly like a long-lost lover, and he did the same, lingering and perhaps wishing it were true.

When they pulled apart, she said, "Sir, we really must go. I have our tickets." She produced them and then slipped them back into her pocket. She was wearing a backpack larger than his, that seemed to be stuffed to capacity.

He smiled. "Lead the way."

She shuffled back outside, and Jake kept pace with her purposeful gait. When they got onto the train, she pushed her way through the crowd like an angry porter.

He followed her toward the back of the train, through the cheap seats, the more private second class compartments, and into a first class sleeper. During the day trips, most of those remained empty because of their price and the fact that most didn't need to sleep during the day. One side of the room had a bench and the other had a bunk bed. Below the window was a small table.

She slung her backpack to the floor, quickly closed the drapes, and turned toward him. Then she reached inside her jacket and pulled out a gun.

"Take off your clothes," she demanded, her expression serious, and her eyes not blinking.

When a woman who looked like her made a firm command like that, he usually complied. The problem was, she had a gun pointing at him. And, although that might be kinky to some, Jake had had a gun pointed at him too many times to count. It never lead to anything sexual.

"Listen," Jake started. "We barely know each other. Maybe we should start off with names. You know mine. Now, what's yours?"

She stood firm, and Jake had a feeling she wasn't messing around. He took off his backpack and started taking off his clothes. When he was down to his socks and underwear, he stopped.

"I haven't had a chance to work out for a few weeks," he said, trying a smile.

Her gun was still pointed at him. "The rest," she said, her gun swishing back and forth at his groin.

He shrugged and slipped off his underwear. Luckily the room wasn't too cold.

"What's this about?" he asked.

"Turn around," she said.

He did what she said, making sure she didn't move toward him at that moment. Instead, he heard his clothes scrape across the floor. She was checking out his I.D., he realized, but these were strange methods.

"Okay," she said. "Get dressed."

He turned around, and she had lowered the gun. Her eyes now shot down toward his crotch. She raised her thin eyebrows. Just as he got dressed, the train pulled away from the station and started picking up speed.

"What was that all about?" he asked her.

She was seated now and her gun back under her jacket.

"I was told you had a small tattoo on your right cheek. A picture of rabbit."

"Hey, that's not just any rabbit. That's Bugs himself. A moment of weakness." He thought for a moment. "You could have just had me pull down my pants."

"What fun would that be?" She smiled now, showing imperfect teeth but a true warmth.

"You were checking for wires," he said.

"Can't be too careful."

He sat down on the seat next to her. "You wouldn't happen to have an extra gun. Something a little more reliable than that Russian knock-off of yours."

She smiled and shook her head. "You insult my gun and then ask for one. Typical."

"Actually, I asked for one and then insulted yours. Seriously, though, I feel somewhat naked without mine."

"If police catch you with one, you won't see light of day for years. Bad way to learn Chinese. Good way to catch disease."

Jake laughed. He had a feeling he was going to like... "What's your name?"

"Chang Su. You can call me Su."

"Is that what they called you at American university?" he asked her.

"Yes."

"And where was that?"

"Stanford"

"Impressive. Is that where they recruited you?"

"They?"

"The people you work with now."

"I work for a communications company in Shanghai," she said convincingly. "I'm scouting Manchuria for cell tower placement."

"And that obviously requires a gun." Jake smiled at her.

She hesitated, the wheels of thought processing in her mind. "Your Network has asked me for a few favors over the past couple of years."

"What'd they have on you? And I'm not with the Network."

"Yet, here you are with me."

"You didn't answer my question. What'd they have on you?"

She didn't want to explain anything to him, it was obvious, but for some reason she said, "I took some things in college. My government forced me. My family was in danger."

"Ah...the old Soviet trick. Work for us or we harm the family. What did you take?"

"Does it matter?"

Probably not, he thought. But he was still curious. "Yes, it does. I like to know the person I'm hanging out with, even if she happens to be a double agent."

"That's not fair. You don't know me."

"You work for two countries; that makes you a double agent."

Her expression was as if she had just realized this with his words. A tear streaked her face.

"I'm sorry," he said. "That wasn't nice."

She wiped the tears away and seemed much better in a hurry, as if his words had meant something.

“I was working on software encryption for a class,” she said. “I told my sister in Beijing. She asked for a copy. I didn’t see a problem. I didn’t know she worked for the government. Next thing I know, two Network men throw me in a big car and talk at me all weekend. After that, I send more things to my sister. Things that don’t work.”

“Classic. Disinformation.”

“I didn’t know.” She shook her head emphatically. “Not until later, when I run the program and see it was bogus. Then I tell my sister.”

“Wow.”

“What?”

“That makes you a triple agent.”

She shook her head no. “Only two countries.”

“Two countries; three sets of information. First, the home country expecting you to feed them good stuff. Then the bogus information from the new country passed off as the truth. Then the truth of the bogus info passed on to the original country. In baseball, that’s a triple play. Very rare.”

“You suck!” Tears streamed down her face again.

“I’m sorry,” he said again, placing his hand on her shoulder. “Listen, can we just start over? Hi, my name is Jake.” He held out his hand for her to shake.

She sniffled and then laughed. “Su me.” She laughed louder now. “I mean, I’m Su.”

Jake laughed for the first time in months.

CHAPTER 11

Bend, Oregon

The brown Ford Taurus pulled to the side of the road behind a Chevy Blazer in a quiet subdivision along the Deschutes River. It was just dark enough to require lights, but Agent Drew Fisher had not turned his on as he followed the Trooper carrying Cliff Johansen and the unknown Asian woman.

He had parked about a block back from the house owned by Zack Evans, who had been Cliff Johansen's old college friend at the University of Oregon.

Fisher had called ahead, and sitting in the Blazer in front of him was the special agent in charge of the Central Oregon Network office, Jane Harris. They had never met, but had talked on the phone a few times in the past few hours on the drive up.

Turning off the dome light, Fisher got out, quietly closed the driver's door, and walked up to the Blazer, getting in the passenger side.

He reached across and shook the agent's hand. "Drew Fisher."

"Jane Harris."

She was a small woman, looking more like a marathon runner than someone who might need to mix it up with criminals. Her hair was cut so short in the back, he could see her scalp. Yet, despite her small frame, Fisher noticed her chest was well represented.

"How long ya been here?" Fisher asked.

She checked her watch. "About two hours. Evans works across the river with a law firm."

"Damn, a lawyer?"

"Actually, he's a CPA. The firm deals mostly with businesses in the area. Evans handles their tax division."

"You think he has a clue about his old college buddy?"

She shook her head. "From what you've told me, Cliff Johansen doesn't sound like he confides in anyone."

"True. But guys tell their college friends more than they tell their priest."

She swiveled her head toward the house down the road with the Trooper in the driveway. "Did you run the plates on the Trooper?"

"Rental. Out to a Jill Jones."

"Didn't look like a Jill to me," she said. "Chinese. Maybe Korean."

"Former, I'd guess. The place she was staying in Union City was rented to a company in San Jose. I've got someone checking into that."

She looked concerned. "This information you suspect he took. How important is it?"

"That's the problem," Fisher said, "I'm not sure what he took. The company has access to every aspect of the missile defense system. Cliff's a computer genius. He could get in and out without anyone's knowledge. We have to suspect worst-case."

And that's what had him so anxious. If Cliff Johansen had taken anything at all, he had done it right under his nose. That could get Fisher fired, if not hung out to dry.

♦

Inside the house of Zack Evans, Li and Cliff Johansen had just finished putting their bags in a spare bedroom on the second floor, and were about to make their way downstairs. Remembering her instructions, and how she needed to hurry the process, she hoped this computer nerd would not try to screw with her-literally and figuratively.

"He wasn't surprised to see you," Li said. "Are you sure you didn't tell him you were coming?"

"Positive." Cliff moved closer to her, planting his right hand on her butt. "He seemed very impressed by you."

She ran her thigh against his crotch seductively. "Let's remain focused. You have to get the data tonight."

The two of them headed downstairs and found Zack Evans in the living room watching CNN and drinking a martini. He was a slight man with round spectacles on top of narrow-set eyes. His hair was spiked up with gel and he smiled through one side of his mouth.

"The bar is open," Evans said, raising his glass. "I can make you one of these...shaken, not stirred. Or I've got some of that good local microbrew that I sent you a few weeks ago."

Cliff started off and then stopped. "I'm havin' a beer. Li, what would you like?"

"Soda."

"You got it." He took off.

While he was gone, Li went to the window and glanced out from the edge of the curtain. She had to make this work. Damn! She still needed to find that Abby Road album for the Laughing Dumbass. He could forgive her for not getting the software, she thought, but if she didn't bring back the Beatles. . . she'd pay for that with her flesh.

"Here you go," Cliff said, handing her a glass of coke.

Li and Cliff took seats across from Evans.

"So, what's up?" Evans asked Cliff.

"Wouldn't you like to know?" Cliff smiled and raised his brows.

"Ya dumb ass. I meant what brings you to Bend on a weekday?"

"I knew that." Cliff glanced sideways at Li. "We were sick of the city. I called in sick and said screw it. Road trip!" He yelled the last two words.

Evans gave him a high five. "You da man." His friend nodded his head at Li. "How long you two know each other?"

Cliff waited for her to speak. When she didn't, he said, "About a month. She was my Tai Chi instructor."

"No shit? You gonna kick my ass in slow motion?"

"That's not what it's about," Li said, looking somewhat disturbed. Slow motion, fast motion, it didn't matter to her.

"I'm sorry," Evans said, "I didn't mean to imply..."

"Listen," Cliff broke in. "You should find a class here in Bend. It clears your mind and body and allows you to focus more clearly on what's important."

Evans considered Li more carefully now. "Yeah, I'll have to look into that."

There was dead silence for a moment that lingered longer than anyone expected.

Cliff broke it. "Your server," he started. "I should take a look at it. Make sure everything is working right."

"Right," Evans said, rising to his feet. He went to the kitchen, but continued the conversation. "I'll make another martini...and we'll look into that." A moment later he returned with a martini in one hand and another beer in the other. "Li, I hope you don't mind helping yourself."

"No problem. I was thinking of taking a walk. Plus, I have to get something from the Trooper."

"Excellent."

♦

The two college friends retreated to the office on the second floor, right next to the guest bedroom.

Cliff took a long draw on his beer, finishing about half of it, and then went to the floor and started opening the server case.

"You fuckin' dog," Evans said, kicking his friend in the leg. "You have a hottie like that and you don't tell me?"

By now Cliff had the side of the case open. He didn't look at his friend when he said, "No big deal."

"Yeah, right. The big city boy has all the arm candy he can handle. Man, you're fulla shit."

Cliff started removing some screws and then stopped. He nearly finished his beer with a quick swig. He had forgotten what he needed in the other room. And, he realized, his friend might actually know more about computers than he suspected.

"It's not what you think," Cliff said, getting up from the floor.

"You havin' sex?"

Cliff shrugged. "Yeah."

"Then it's what I think."

"Who's the dog now? Back in a sec."

Cliff went to the bedroom and pulled out an external DVD burner from his bag, along with two blank DVD-Rs. Then he returned to the office, where he found his friend peering inside the server case.

"That a whole lotta wires and shit," Evans said. "Give me numbers and figures any day."

"Get the hell outta my way," Cliff said playfully. "Man on a mission." He finished his beer and set the bottle on the desk.

Cliff hitched up his DVD burner, plugging it into a FireWire port. He could have accessed the server from his home in California and transferred the data back to his drive there, but he didn't want anyone to be able to trace it back to him. He could have also burned a copy from there and handed it over to Li, but then she could have screwed him out of the money. He had to stick with his plan, even though it wasn't the easiest way to do things.

In a moment he found his hidden files and started transferring them to his blank DVD. While he did this, he encrypted the files with a 512 bit scheme he had developed himself. Even if someone got their hands on the files, there would be no way they could break his codes.

"This won't take much longer," Cliff said. "Could you get me another beer?"

Just as his friend left the room, he heard the door downstairs close.

One more copy, he thought, and then they'd go to the bank in the morning. Smooth as a baby's ass.

♦

"There you go," Special Agent Fisher said. "The Asian woman."

"Should we haul her ass in?" Harris said, her eyes on the woman, who had just gone to the Trooper and was now walking down the sidewalk in the opposite direction.

"We have nothing on her."

"What about probable cause to believe she's in the act of committing espionage against our country?"

Fisher smiled. "I meant something real."

She raised her head as she said, "So that's how we're gonna operate. I just like to lay down the ground rules."

"For now. But keep asking."

CHAPTER 12

The train to Harbin was slow and plodding and expected to take all day to travel the five hundred miles or so, stopping in nearly ever one-water-buffalo town to drop off and pick up passengers.

Jake Adams watched Chang Su as she slept on the lower bunk, the constant sway of the train almost lulling him as well. It should have, he thought, since he had barely slept on the train from Beijing to Shenyang the night before.

She woke now and caught him watching her. "Was I making noise?" she asked, pulling her legs to the floor and sitting up. She ran her fingers through her dark, straight hair, brushing it away from her eyes.

"No," Jake said. "I was thinking I should be doing the same thing." He thought about his current task, and wondered if she had the same information. He knew how the Network liked to compartmentalize everything on a need to know basis. The military had been even more restrictive in that regard.

Time for a fishing expedition.

"Tell me the plan," he said.

"The plan?"

"What we do after we get to Harbin?"

She looked confused. "They should have told you."

They had told him, but that wasn't the point. "I'm a civilian. I was in Beijing as a personal security officer for an American businessman. I was asked if I would help. That's it."

"I thought you were Network."

"At one time, yes. But that was years ago, before the Network existed."

"Why you here, then?"

"Like I said. A favor."

She hesitated, in deep thought. "This is pretty dangerous for a favor."

That's not what he wanted to hear. He had left those dangerous missions behind. At least that's what he thought.

"After Harbin?" he probed.

"You serious?" She shook her head. "We go to northern frontier. Less than hundred miles from Russia. You need better clothes. We get that in Harbin."

"What's there?" he asked, knowing the answer. At least hoping he did. It wouldn't have been the first time he had been lied to on a mission.

"A mobile missile base. Very high security. We can hit Moscow, New Delhi, Los Angeles, Seattle from there. Soon even New York with newer weapons."

What the hell was going on? He was told they would be checking into laser weapons.

"That's pretty well known," Jake said. "I read a story about those in Newsweek."

"What's your point?"

"Tell me something I don't know."

"How do I know what you don't know? I don't even know what you know." She smiled now.

He was starting to like her.

"I'm sure we have all kinds of satellite photos of that location, right down to the damn serial numbers on the side of each missile. What more do they need?"

She shrugged. "I just do what I'm told. I get a call, meet Network man, and he tells me to take a few days off. I tell my real job I have to visit my sick sister in Xi'an."

"This the same sister who made you a triple agent?"

"I'm not triple agent." She looked genuinely concerned or angry. "Same sister, though."

"Does she live in Xi'an?"

"Used to...but I haven't seen her in a year. She moves a lot."

Jake needed to get her back on track, but he didn't want to push her too hard. "So we go to the missile base in the north," he said. "Then what? Just waltz in and snap a few shots? What's the point? And why are you helping?"

Her jaw tightened and Jake thought for a moment that she was ready to pull her gun again.

"China doesn't need more missiles. We need food for our people."

"And cell phones." Jake smiled at her.

"Right. Gotta keep in touch with family. China is big, Jake. It's easier to set up cell towers than to run phone lines to every remote province. We skip a step."

Jake couldn't argue with that point. It wouldn't be long before they ripped up all hard phone lines worldwide.

Suddenly the train lurched, thrusting Su to the floor and shoving Jake back into his seat. He helped her up, and then went to the window and peered outside. They had either hit something, or the conductor had hit the brakes hard, because they were now slowing fast and coming to a halt.

"What's going on?" she asked, sliding her head around him.

The train had now come to a complete stop.

Su had a grave expression as she turned away from the window, closing the drapes.

"What's the matter?" Jake asked.

"I saw police cars," she said. "And military vehicles. On the cross road ahead."

"And?"

"It means they're looking for someone."

"I've done nothing wrong. Except deviate from my visa itinerary. But nobody knows about that." He looked at her. "What about you?"

"I've done nothing."

"You've worked for the government before," he said. "Are you sure they haven't been watching you? What about your meeting with the Network man prior to leaving Shanghai?"

She shook her head emphatically. "I have secure cell phone." She rummaged through her bag to produce the most advanced cell phone Jake had ever seen. "It's coded nowhere. I route through six cities randomly. Only one man has the number."

"The Network man. Who's that?"

Before she could answer, there was a great commotion at the front of their car, with loud voices.

"What's going on?" Jake asked.

She didn't answer. Instead, she pulled out her gun and her eyes shifted about the small compartment.

"Wipe it clean," Jake said, moving to the window. He peaked through the edge of the curtain and saw soldiers making their way alongside the tracks. Two of them, side by side. "Damn!"

The voices were getting closer. Jake thought about what he had in his own bag that could be scrutinized. He had the camera and the phone that would transmit the photos. He had memorized the numbers to call, so that wouldn't be a problem. Think. What else? He had nothing, and maybe that was the problem. He didn't even have a proper coat for the climate, yet he was traveling without real luggage to a city with no real tourist attractions with a woman he barely knew. Was this an elaborate set up? He didn't think so, but worse things had happened to him in the past. The gun. It had to go.

He looked back outside. The two men had passed. Their backs were to the window now.

"Give me the gun." Jake put on some leather gloves and took it from her. "Any extra clips or loose rounds?"

Embarrassed, she retrieved a full clip from her backpack. Jake took that also, wiped her prints from it, and checked the window again.

The voices were now at the compartment next door. Someone down the hall laughed for a long moment and then it stopped with the slam of a door.

Jake opened the window and poked his head outside, looking both ways. All clear. Then he thought and checked the gun to make sure there was no round chambered. The first round was in the clip. Good. He stepped back and launched the gun outside. It landed near some tall weeds in a foot of snow.

"Hurry," she said. "They're coming."

Jake threw the clip and it too sunk into the snow. Then he closed the window and took a seat next to Su, who held his hand.

There was a sharp knock on the door, followed by the door swinging in swiftly. A semi-gray man with short hair, wearing a police uniform and holding an automatic handgun, shifted his eyes about the small compartment. Behind him stood three younger officers with automatic assault carbines drawn. Behind them, barely visible, was a bald man in civilian clothes.

The man in charge focused his gaze on Su and asked her something in Chinese. She looked disturbed by the question, but she didn't answer. Instead, she slid her bag across the floor toward him.

He holstered his gun and immediately started rifling through her stuff.

When he found her cell phone, he stopped and looked it over carefully.

He asked her about it, and Jake assumed he must have found something intriguing about that phone because he started punching buttons.

"What's he doing?" Jake whispered to Su.

"Nothing," she said, shaking her head.

The man in charge cast his eyes on Jake. "You American? Passport!"

Jake hesitated and saw the man's hand move toward his gun. Reaching inside his jacket, Jake retrieved his passport and handed it to the officer in charge.

The man flipped through pages and found Jake's visa, which was a concern to him, since his contact in Russia had hastily provided it only two days ago.

Changing expressions from curious to concern, the officer raised his brows. "Say Beijing here," the man said. "Nothing about Harbin."

Su said something in Chinese and then followed up in English with, "We met and I want you to see Chinese countryside." Su let out a breath. She was concerned.

The man had Jake's passport in one hand and the cell phone in the other. He seemed to be trying to make a connection, but nothing was registering.

Without great fanfare, the officer spouted off a series of words that Jake didn't understand. Then he handed him his passport and stuffed her phone back in her bag. They were gone just as quickly as they had entered.

"What the hell was that all about?" Jake asked her.

"He a...what you say? Asshole?"

Jake laughed at the way it came from her lips. "As you know, we have those in America as well. I meant, what did he say before leaving?"

"He bitch at me, saying I should know to update visa before taking American to other places."

"What are they looking for?"

"They say a man who killed two people in Shenyang."

Now Jake wished they had simply hidden the gun somewhere in the compartment. This wasn't America, where he could find a gun easily, or even Europe, where he had guns placed in various cities of almost each country, just in case he needed one. He had no reason to believe he'd need a gun, but he also knew that circumstances often lead in that direction.

CHAPTER 13

Shemya, Alaska

Standing at the edge of the 300-foot-high cliff, the constant wind making it nearly impossible to stand, the man glanced out onto a dark Pacific Ocean. He wrapped his arms around his trunk and shivered. Two months ago he had been in the Bay Area, where, although cold and windy much of the time, was no comparison to this, he thought. Whoever thought about stationing the military here should have been shot, and yet he had volunteered for the assignment when Brightstar needed an electrical engineer to help with their contract, where they would bring online the newest early warning radar for the missile defense system.

That was the plan. But he was an entrepreneur. Always had been, since his youth when he ran a network of paper boys like a pimp with whores, taking a cut of each paycheck.

No. When someone shoved a boatload of money in front of him, he had taken two seconds to say "hell yeah."

He checked his watch. It was time. He pulled the backpack from his back and retrieved a satellite phone. In a few seconds, he had the phone set up and the number punched in.

"Yeah, it's me." He hesitated and glanced about him. "Right, I'm standin' in the middle of the mess hall."

He listened now, his expression changing from playful to grave. Trying to say something several times, he was cut off before a single word slipped out.

"Yes, I understand. I'm sorry. It's not a problem."

Shaking his head, he clicked off the phone and returned it to the bag.

Then he sealed it in a camouflaged water-tight case and hid it among the low scrub brush. Only the occasional blue fox would know it was there.

♦

Cliff Johansen cleared the empty beer bottles into a recycle bin. He remembered from his college days that each bottle was worth five cents, so he and Zack Evans had stacked the 12-packs up as furniture in their apartment in Eugene until they were short on cash. He laughed to himself with the thought, considering his current salary and the payoff he was about to receive.

"What's so funny?" Li asked, coming into the kitchen.

"Nothing. Just thinking of our college days. Now Zack drinks more martinis than beer."

"Did Zack go to bed?"

"Yeah, he has to work in the morning."

She looked behind her, toward the living room and beyond, and then back toward Cliff. "You get everything?"

Nice try, he thought. "I told you I put it in both places. No remote access. I got half."

Moving her body next to him, she said, "Then you get half. What you want? Upper or lower?"

Cliff was excited now, realizing he would get it at least one more time. She was the sweetest lay he'd ever had, and probably the best he could hope to have for some time. Anything he could do to delay the inevitable would be great with him.

He reached behind and planted his hand on her butt, pulling her closer to him, hoping she would feel his excitement.

"I guess I got my answer," she said. "Let's go. We have work to do in the morning."

Cliff followed her through the house and up the stairs, his eyes not moving from her fine ass.

CHAPTER 14

Harbin, China

It was closing in on midnight by the time the train made it into the main Harbin station. Jake knew the delay could have been much worse, but it was disturbing that they had lost nearly four hours with the police searching their train from one side to the other.

After getting off the train, Jake and Chang Su had taken a cab to within a few blocks of the apartment of her contact, whom she had worked with a couple of times in the past, and the guy who would drive them north in the morning.

Cruising along the downtown streets in the cab, it was easy for Jake to see the Russian influence to Harbin, with the onion domes splattered across the skyline. Sidewalks were covered with snow, and those who were still walking about at that hour, were bundled in thick layers of clothing, clouds of breath streaming out with each quick step.

Jake was still under-dressed with his leather jacket. He guessed the temperature was somewhere around ten below zero; colder than normal for February, according to his local guide.

Su must have seen him shiver. "We get you a warm coat in the morning."

"How much farther?"

"Not far."

Shortly the cab pulled over to a curb in a run-down residential section. The cabbie had parked in front of a bar. She paid the man and they both got out to the sidewalk.

"You want a drink?" Jake asked.

"No, we should go. We're already hours late." She started off down the sidewalk, the large backpack over her shoulders.

"Well, I could have used a beer," he said, following her.

They had gone about a block when she stopped and moved into the shadows.

"What?" Jake whispered.

"His car is gone." She pointed up the pavement and across the street. "He always parks it there."

"Maybe it's in the shop," Jake said. "What's this guy do?"

"Computer programmer. We were at Stanford together."

"You say he knows you're coming? Maybe we missed him at the train station. Let's check it out."

She held his arm, stopping him. A car rounded the corner from behind, its lights shining on them. She wrapped her arm around his waist and pulled him to her. The car drove slowly down the block and turned right.

Now Jake was starting to believe her that something was wrong. There had been two men in that car, trying their best not to glare at the two of them.

"Now," she said, separating from him and crossing the street.

They entered a dark stairwell from the street and started climbing the cement steps. Slowly. Methodically. Jake checked his back with each step.

At the top of the stairs, she stopped and gazed down the dark corridor, lit only by a single bulb about halfway down. Jake noticed the concern on her face, even more so than when the police checked the train earlier in the day.

She reached inside her coat and then shook her head, realizing her gun was gone.

They stepped forward quietly.

"Which apartment?" Jake whispered.

She nodded her head toward the door on the left. Almost knocking with her leather-gloved hand, she hesitated and tried the door latch. The door swung in.

She gasped with the sight of the trashed room. There were papers and items of clothing strewn about the floor. Seat cushions were ripped apart. And it was worse when she hit the light.

There in the center of the floor, naked, lay a man on his stomach. His body was bruised and cut, with a pool of blood seeping from each side of his upper torso.

Su immediately wept, but tried her best to hold back her pain. Keep from crying out. Setting her backpack on the floor, she knelt down at the man's side, her hand over her mouth.

"Su, we've gotta leave," Jake urged softly. "Let's go!"

She said nothing, her face turning from anguish to shock.

Jake grabbed her and pulled her to her feet. He slung her bag over one shoulder and led her into the corridor with his free hand.

Just then he heard tires screech to a halt outside, followed by doors opening.

Glancing about the hallway, there was only one choice. They had to run to the end of the hall.

"Come on," he said to her firmly.

Together they lumbered down the corridor. Jake hit the light as he passed, smashing it to the floor.

At the end of the hall, there was another stairway. As they reached the bottom of the stairs, Jake heard the sound of footsteps running outside. He swung her backpack around and caught the first man in the face, knocking him back into the next man and back outside. Then Jake rushed them, kicking one in the face as he tried to rise.

Jake led her down the street and quickly turned right down an alley. Her expression had changed from pain and sorrow to anger. Determined now, she took her backpack from Jake and slung it over her shoulders.

"This way," she said, decidedly.

She went down a narrow passageway and eventually they slowed their pace to silence their movement.

Soon they reached a park along the Songhua River and headed toward downtown. Before exiting the other end of the park, Su stopped and went to her knees in the snow alongside a patch of bushes. She cried and hid her face from Jake's view.

"You were close?" Jake asked, his hand on her shoulder.

She didn't answer. He looked around and realized they had left tracks in the snow.

"Listen, Su," he said. "We've gotta get out of town. That was a major set-up."

Finally she spoke. "Why?"

Jake gently squeezed her shoulder. "Someone wanted you in custody. Out of the way."

"But it makes no sense," she said, weeping. "All they know is we're friends from college."

"You've been compromised," Jake said.

She glared up at him. "I killed him," she muttered.

"No."

"I did. I got him into this in college."

"It's not your fault."

She shook her head.

Damn it. They needed to move fast before the police had a chance to close off the city. He pulled her roughly from the ground and shook her.

"I need you right now," he said sternly. "Now get your ass in gear and move it."

She looked as if he had just slapped her in a Buddhist temple. But she did what he said.

Together they moved toward downtown. When they got to a main road, they picked up a bus that brought them toward the train station. They watched with horror as they approached the station. There were three cop cars lined up outside, with officers watching the front door.

Jake had no intention of jumping on a train anyway, but his plans would have to change nonetheless. They continued on the bus for a while until they reached an area with many bars and restaurants. They got off and stood for a moment alongside the street.

"Now what?" Su asked.

"There." Jake shifted his eyes toward the cab parked a half a block away.

"Are you sure?"

"Just keep your ears open." Jake tried to remember a map he had viewed on the train before entering the city. "Make up an address along Anguo Street. Make it out a ways."

She nodded and they got into the cab.

The cabbie considered him with interest. Apparently he wasn't used to seeing Americans. He pulled away and seemed to be flying through the nearly empty streets.

It wasn't long before they caught up with Anguo Street, which connected the southwest section of town to the downtown.

When they had reached an area that was mostly smaller buildings, the cab pulled over to the side of the road.

Su started to get out, but Jake stopped her. Instead, he got out on the driver's side, opened the driver's door and pulled the man to the street. Then, with the car still running, Jake jumped in and sped away.

Glancing in the rearview mirror, Jake watched Su in the back, stunned and shaking her head.

"You're crazy," she said. "He got a good look at you."

Leaving her backpack behind, she climbed to the front seat.

"Nah. We all look alike." Besides, he had a feeling the cops knew exactly who they were look for now. Jake took it slow, remembering from his map that there should be a road ahead that led toward the main north and south highway in Manchuria.

"What about me?" she asked.

"They already know what you look like. You were set up big time."

She thought hard. "But why?"

"Your friend must have given you up." As soon as he said it, Jake regretted having done so.

"Bullshit!" The word came from her mouth, but she made it sound more like a French soup than an expletive.

He couldn't help but laugh to himself. But she still caught him.

"You think it's funny my friend is killed?"

"No. I'm sorry. It's just the way you say Bullshit."

The road ahead looked about right, so Jake turned right onto it and picked up speed.

Time to heal the situation. Jake said, "I am truly sorry about your friend. And, we can't be sure he gave you up, but he was obviously tortured. I certainly couldn't blame him if he did."

She considered that. "Doesn't matter. It's over."

"What's over?"

"Our job," she said, defeated. "You might as well go back to Beijing, catch a flight back to Europe."

Jake smiled. "You obviously don't know me very well."

She shrugged. "They say you pig-headed and...what's that word? Obstacle? Obnoxious? No, that's not it."

"Maybe..."

"No I'll get it. Give me a second." The wheels were turning fast now. "Obsessed. No."

Jake found the main highway and headed in the direction of Qiqihar. He wasn't sure if they should stay on the main road, but for now it was the fastest way out of town.

“Obstinate,” she said proudly. “That’s the word.”

“I’ve been called worse,” he said. “Still, we’ve gotta assume they know about you. Your friend didn’t know about me, right?”

She shook her head.

“But it won’t take the cops long to figure it out. The cop on the train got both of our names. If he’s got a halfway decent memory....”

Her concern registered again on her expressive face.

All the more reason to get the hell off the main road, Jake thought. First, he’d need to figure out if their mission was remotely possible now. If her friend had given up Su, he could have just as easily told them that he would be driving her to the remote location. Hopefully that’s all he had known.

♦

Outside the contact’s apartment, police cars had blocked off the street and two men were carrying the man out on a stretcher, down the front steps and into an unmarked military van.

Leaning against a police car, bundled in a parka, the bald man cast his gaze on an army colonel in a green wool uniform standing before him.

“I’m sorry, sir,” the colonel said, his eyes and head nodding toward the street.

The bald man laughed, his voice echoing against the apartments, breaking the silence of night. Then his disposition changed to a determined stare.

“You are the Fool on the Hill,” the bald man said. “I am the Walrus. Goo goo g’ joob.”

The colonel looked at him like he was insane.

The bald man continued, “It doesn’t matter. Luckily I don’t depend entirely on you.” In fact, he did not depend on the colonel at all, or anyone else in the military of incompetents. But he knew he would need them eventually, when his plan came to full fruition. So, even though he did not like it at all, he would have to appease this colonel. For now.

The bald man moved off of the police car and put his hand on the colonel’s shoulder board, running his fingers through the stars. “Let’s sanitize the apartment. He was a troubled young man. Suicidal, in fact.” Then a smile came to his face and a chuckle turned in to a full gaffaw.

CHAPTER 15

Bend, Oregon

It was Friday morning and Special Agent Jane Harris stood at a table in the downtown branch of the Bank of the Pacific, pretending to fill out a form, and taking her time about it. Sitting at a small table a short distance away, Cliff Johansen and the Asian woman talked with a bank official. But she was just out of ear shot.

Moments later, Cliff signed something and then went with the banker into the vault. The Asian women glanced about the room, checking her watch every now and then.

Harris knew she couldn't stay there much longer. She was being too obvious. She had to move. Picking up some literature on a bank credit card, she went to an open teller and asked her a few questions about their current rates. Then she smiled and left, returning to her vehicle parked half a block from the Trooper.

"Well?" asked agent Drew Fisher. "What's up?"

"The two of them talked for a moment with a banker and then Cliff went into the vault without her."

"Probably a safe deposit box."

"That's what I was thinking."

"What else?" he asked her.

"Current Visa rates are nine percent. I might apply."

He gave her a callous look.

"All right. Give me a break. It's not like I got much sleep in this beast of a Blazer last night. Cliff did fill out some paperwork."

"Wire transfer?"

"Could be."

"I'll call and have that traced."

"What about probable cause now?" she asked. "Last night..."

He waved her off. "You wanna sleep in here again?"

"Carry on."

He called Portland and initiated a trace. Just as he got off the phone, he noticed Cliff and the woman departing the bank.

"Here we go," Fisher said.

Agent Harris started the engine and waited for them to pull out.

♦

Li was behind the wheel of the Trooper and Cliff sat in the passenger seat, squirming about nervously.

"You act like we just robbed the bank," she said, checking the rearview mirror as she pulled out into traffic. "You should be happy. You're half a million richer."

Cliff sighed with her words, as if he had finally just realized what she was saying. On one point she was correct. He did have more money. But he was now also culpable for a crime. He had stolen from his country and sold the data to this woman who worked for...well, that was the problem. He assumed it was the Chinese government, but it could have been the Taiwanese, the Koreans, North or South, or even some terrorist group. And the DVD he had just given her was useless without his encryption codes.

They made their way toward the Parkway that led out of town. She turned North toward Redmond and picked up speed, keeping her eyes on the rearview mirror.

"What's the matter," he asked her.

"I think someone's behind us."

"A tail?" He looked over his shoulder and saw at least five vehicles. "Which one?"

"Turn around," she said. "Don't want them to know we know."

A moment later she looped around and picked up Highway 20 toward Sisters. But the Blazer with the two people were still there.

Cliff leaned forward and looked into the right outside mirror. "The Blazer?" he asked.

"Yeah."

She passed a long line of cars before the highway turned from four lanes to two. Now there would be a little cushion.

The road quickly became a series of curves that would not allow passing.

"Listen," Cliff said, "what difference does it make? So we've got a tail. What do they have on us?"

She glanced sideways at him, a look he had not seen in her before. What was it? Desperation? Concern?

When she spoke, her words were measured. "We have the DVD you just gave me. We have the transfer of money you just got. We have you not showing up for work for the last two days. And, how we sure you not get caught sending data to yourself?"

That was the only thing he was sure of, but she was right about the rest. Well, not the money. For, although she had transferred the money to his local account, he had set it up days ago to have all of his transactions, however small or large, split into fractions of one hundred. So, a transfer of one dollar would look like one cent. Subsequently, a transfer of five hundred thousand, would end up as one hundred transfers of five thousand each, keeping it well under the ten thousand dollars that would send up flags with the Feds. He smiled now thinking of his own genius. Not only would the incoming money be fractionalized, it would immediately shift before the end of business to five other accounts in various sheltered countries. And, over a period of a few days, the money would again collect in a single account in Liechtenstein.

"What so funny?" she asked him.

"Nothing. This is just getting so cloak and dagger. It's pretty cool."

"Glad you like it."

When a passing lane came up, she sped up and started to pass a slow-moving camper trailer. But then she slowed down when she was even with the camper. Just before the passing lane was about to end, she jammed the gas and passed the truck and camper, barely making it with the oncoming traffic honking at her. Now the line of cars, with the Blazer at the end, would be even farther behind.

She sped up and rushed toward the small town of Sisters.

♦

"Damn it!" said special agent Harris. "She's on to us."

Agent Fisher had his hand on the dash. "Looks like it." He pulled out a map from a side pouch and opened it to their current location. "Shit. The road splits in Sisters to one twenty-six and two forty-two. Which way will they go?"

"No. The McKenzie Highway, two forty-two, is closed until June or July. But that's not the big problem. Look down the road a ways. Twenty splits to twenty-two toward Salem, they could stay on twenty toward Corvallis, or they could shoot down on one twenty-six to Eugene."

Fisher let out a heavy sigh. "Fuck. I'm gonna guess Eugene, since Cliff has another good friend there and he went to college there. But we need to get some help on the road from our friends." He pulled out his cell phone and punched in a Portland number.

He talked for a while, making sure there was a state patrol car watching for a white Trooper with California plates on Highway 22, Highway 20, and Highway 126, prior to any turn-offs. Once that was set, he made sure they had a Eugene police unit sitting on Cliff's friend's place there.

"Well?" she asked. "Now what?"

"We bust our ass to Eugene. We'll get no Network help there. The entire office is in Portland at an organized anarchist rally."

"That's right. I was supposed to be there, but got pulled off for this gig."

"You can thank me any time," he said. "Oh yeah, we'll need to change cars in Eugene. You don't find that strange?"

"Changing cars?"

"No. Organized anarchists. Kind of a contradiction."

She smiled. "Guess so."

They pushed on ahead, passing as many cars as they could at each opportunity.

CHAPTER 16

Northern Manchuria

Jake had driven the taxi most of the night to Qiqihar. Since it had been so cold, with the heater barely working, they had been forced to keep their gloves on for the entire trip, which made it easy to clean up before dumping the car in front of a park some six blocks from the train station. They would have left no fingerprints.

Now they were on a rickety old train used mostly by locals or the military, judging by all those in uniform, heading farther north into the hinterlands bordering Manchuria, Inner Mongolia, and Russia just a short distance over a mountain range.

Although the train traveled along a river valley, mountains rose up from the east and west and seemed to be drawing to a close ahead, Jake noticed. There were no private compartments on this commuter, only rows of shabby chairs.

The sun was rising and Su sat next to him, her head against his shoulder. She woke now and noticed Jake watching her.

"Where are we?" she whispered to him.

He shrugged. "I don't know. My map isn't very detailed."

She looked outside and saw the sun making its way to the top of the mountain on the right side of the train. Then she looked to the left.

"Those are the Hinggan Mountains," she said, closing her eyes slightly and yawning.

"How can you tell?"

"First, my grandfather worked here when I was a child. I came to visit him each summer. Might have been on this very train. Second, my company built a communications site on the ridge last year."

"For the army?"

She glanced around the car at the dozing soldiers. "For our government. Why do you think I'm here?" she said more quietly.

"How far?"

She looked around and then got up, pulling Jake along until they reached the back of the car. Pulling the door open, they went between two cars. The noise from metal wheels against metal rails would drown out their voices.

Finally, she turned and said, "They're not used to hearing English this far north."

"Hey, I'm just a tourist," he said. "You're my tour guide." Part of him believed that, but another part, the more realistic part, knew that the authorities in Harbin would put the word out that Su was traveling with an American man. "You're right. We'll need to get off this train soon or face a search like the last one. And this time they'll actually be looking for us."

She looked out at the countryside passing by. There where tall fir forests, the frost glistening on the needles with the rising sun.

"There's a small village ahead. The next stop. We can get off there. That leaves us ten miles from Nenjiang. The soldiers will get off there and ride by bus to the site."

"How far is that?"

"They go another ten miles into the mountains. They reach a...what you call it in English?" She searched her mind. "Platter?"

"Plateau?"

"Yes, a plateau, surrounded on all sides by mountains. Very isolated. Only one road in."

"How do we get there?" he asked.

"We cut off angle from northwest, then travel over the mountain through the forest."

Jake looked out the window. The mountains were quite snowy, but they didn't seem very tall. They reminded him of Oregon's coast range. The difference? It had to be below zero out there.

He was wearing short hiking boots; more like high top basketball shoes with deep treads. Those wouldn't work under these conditions.

"I need some different clothes," he said.

"I've got that covered," she assured him, smiling.

They went back into the car with the soldiers and took a seat.

A short while later the train slowed and came to a halt in the small village. As suspected, the soldiers stayed put while Jake and Su casually got off the train and walked into the little town. The air was bitter cold, with a slight breeze sweeping down from the mountains to the west. There was no real downtown. There was a small restaurant attached to a tiny market where, invariably, most people in town would get their food. There was one gas pump that sat alongside the road, and, according to Su, a man would come out from his house when the rare car needed fuel.

They walked along trying not to stand out, but not being able to hide Jake much. He was, after all, wearing clothes that would never be found in that part of Manchuria, and Jake assumed he was probably at least five or six inches taller than the average man there.

He was freezing. The wind whipped right through his thin clothes as if they were made of rice paper.

"What about a change of clothes?" Jake asked her.

She didn't lose stride. Instead, she lifted her chin slightly and said, "Just ahead."

They were almost out of town now and Jake noticed the train pulling away, steaming toward the north.

Su turned down a small road that lead to a single house with smoke streaming from a chimney. When they reached the front door, she hesitated, glancing sideways at Jake.

"What?" Jake said.

She sighed. "I'm afraid."

"Afraid of what?"

She thought for a moment. "They found my friend. What if they know about this place?"

"Could they know? Did you plan on coming here?"

She shook her head.

"Did you tell your friend about this place?"

She shook her head again. "No. But he did know about it. It's my uncle. I talked about him, but we weren't supposed to come here."

"Then you should be all right," Jake said.

Reassured, she knocked lightly on the door. Nothing. She was about to knock again, when the door swung open. Standing there was a man in his early sixties, with hair to his shoulders. His mustache, gray and black, hung down to his chin on both sides. Surprisingly, he was as tall as Jake.

There was a long series of conversation as the man escorted them into his house. They took chairs near the fireplace, and Jake could finally start to feel the skin on his face. In a moment, the conversation seemed to move toward him, since Su was looking at him with her arm extending toward him.

The old man reached his hand out toward Jake and they shook briefly, which Jake knew was out of tradition for China. Then the uncle got up and went to a small kitchen area, leaving the two of them alone.

"Does he speak English?" Jake asked her.

"Not a word," she said smiling.

"What did you tell him?"

"I said you were an old college friend. You wanted to see my homeland, where I spent much of my youth. He's very happy. They don't see Americans here."

"That could be a problem. You'll have to tell him not to mention us to the people in town."

"I didn't think about that," she said. "Problem is, most of the town probably saw us come here."

CHAPTER 17

The drive from sunny Central Oregon had gradually turned to sprinkles and then to a steady downpour by the time agents Fisher and Harris had reached Eugene.

An Oregon Highway Patrol officer, sitting among the thick forest on a side road, had spotted the white Trooper with California plates five miles east of Springfield and had followed it at a distance into Eugene, where they had turned it over to an unmarked police unit. That car had followed the Trooper to the western edge of town to the home of James Patterson, an old college friend of Cliff Johansen. An office worker for the Network's Eugene office had delivered a brown Ford Taurus to the agents, taking the Chevy Blazer in return.

The two of them sat now in the Taurus two blocks down from Patterson's house in a subdivision of newer homes watching the driveway through a rain-smeared windshield.

"What are we doing?" Harris asked, running her hands through her hair to remove as much rain as she could. "You see, this is why I live across the mountains."

Fisher's eyes remained on the white Trooper. "I thought you were from Seattle originally. Should be used to this shit."

"Doesn't mean I have to like it," she said. "Now what?"

"Now we wait."

Fisher's cell phone jangled a familiar song from the 80s, so he quickly flipped it open and said, "Fisher." He listened carefully for some time. Then he said "Thanks," and slammed it shut. He looked across at Harris, who had a quizzical expression. "What?"

"Barry Manilow?" she said, smiling.

"I've been trying to change it for weeks. Do you want to know what Portland has to say?"

"Yes, please."

"Cliff got a large transfer of money from a Cayman account."

"How much?"

"Half a mil."

She let out a little whistle. "Let's go. We've got him."

"Maybe. But the money disappeared."

She looked confused. "What?"

"The money was there, and then it wasn't. They say it was split into pieces and sent elsewhere."

"How many pieces?"

"At least a hundred."

"That's proof enough," she said. "He's trying to hide it."

"Right. We can get him on tax evasion a little over a year from now when he fails to report the income. But first we'd have to find it and put all the pieces back together again. Damn it!" He shook his head and stared at the rain hitting the windshield.

"I thought he wasn't this smart," she said.

"I never said that. I said he had left a trail...not a huge trail, though. I guessed he was in it for the sex. Now I'm not so sure. But he is a brilliant programmer. There's no doubt about that."

"So, where will the money end up?"

He shrugged. "I would transfer it into another currency or buy up gold. Maybe bonds. Have it held in Europe."

"The Swiss are out. I'd guess Luxemburg or Liechtenstein. They're less obvious."

He smiled. "Or he could have it routed right back into the same bank in the Caymans. Regardless, they'll track it down."

Harris leaned forward to wipe the windshield where fog had built up. "I say we haul his ass in. Let me take a shot at that geek."

"We have nothing on him officially."

"Bullshit! The guy takes off from work for two days without mentioning it to his boss. We know someone transferred some data for at least thirty seconds. Then we have Cliff taking half a million bucks and trying to hide the money. Damn. That's more probable cause than we had on Walker."

"True. But with Walker we at least knew who was paying him. We need to know who this Asian woman works for, otherwise we have nothing."

"Great. Then let me have her alone for a while."

He smiled with that thought, his eyes penetrating the rain and focused on the Trooper.

♦

Inside James Patterson's house, Cliff sat at the kitchen counter watching his old friend make hamburger's on the stove.

"This is one helluva surprise, Cliff," Patterson said, his attention on his cooking. "Man, I wish you had called. I only have a couple of beers in the house. Shit, we can head on down and pick up some Steelhead. Just like old times. You sure she doesn't want a burger? Man, you gotta put some meat on her bones." He glanced back around looking for Li. "Where'd she go?"

"She's probably doing some Tai Chi in the bedroom," Cliff said.

Patterson reached down and shook his substantial belly. "She can have some a this shit." Then he flipped the burgers and plopped a thick piece of cheese on each. Cliff's old friend leaned toward him. "How'd you meet such a hottie?" he whispered.

"She came to our work to teach a few Tai Chi lessons. Management thought we'd be more productive if we were more relaxed. We kind of hit it off, so she gave me her card and said to come to lessons. Turns out she lived and taught on the east bay close to me."

"One thing leads to the next," Patterson said. "You dog. You always did have a thing for Asian chicks. Not that ya got any." He turned and pulled the burgers from the pan, setting them gingerly onto buns. "No fries. Just chips."

He turned and put the plate down in front of his friend. After a few minutes of silent munching, the food was devoured.

"How do you like working at home?" Cliff asked him.

"It's cool. As you know, you can do websites anywhere. Makes it nice when old college buds show up outta the blue." He smiled broadly.

"I'm sorry I didn't call, man. My bad."

"No problemo. But I expect all the sordid details."

Cliff smiled, but his smirk quickly changed as he saw Li enter the room. She had an automatic pistol with a silencer pointed at his head.

CHAPTER 18

Shemya, Alaska

Colonel Powers shuffled across the frozen sidewalk toward the command post. The snow from the night before had mostly blown in strips of one-foot drifts every ten feet. A young airman was just finishing clearing a path.

"Sorry it's taking so long, Sir," the airman said. "The snow blower blew a belt yesterday. I'll have it fixed by the end of the day."

"No problem, John. Looks good." The colonel entered the building and approached a check point with two security police behind a locked cage. Everything at this base was low tech from first glance and would have to be upgraded before it became operational again. For now, though, it would have to do, the colonel thought. It was more important to make sure the new technology, including the upgraded software, worked as advertised. And, he knew, security was much easier to maintain when he knew every person on a first-name basis.

"Hey, guys," the colonel said, pulling his entry badge and I.D. card from inside his parka. "If John slips on the ice out there, you make sure to haul his ass inside. Fifteen minutes out there without moving and he's dead."

"You got it, Sir," said the sergeant in charge. "Sir, you don't have to show us those. We know who you are."

"My orders," Colonel Powers said. "No one enters without proper I.D., entry badge, and they have to be on the list."

The door buzzed and the colonel entered, the sergeant closing the metal cage behind him.

"Kinda like my New York club," the large airman said.

"That's right," Colonel Powers said, his hand on the man's shoulder. "You're the bouncer."

"Have a good one, Sir," the sergeant said to the colonel's back.

Colonel Powers walked to the end of the corridor, punched in a four-number code on the cipher lock and then entered, heading down a flight of stairs to a basement shelter. The command post was set up to withstand any conventional attack and everything but a direct nuclear strike. The air was filtered and self contained, and there was enough food and water in there to last more than a month.

At the bottom of the stairs was a series of two doors. The first was controlled by a cipher lock, which the colonel went through. The second was shielded and sealed from inside.

The colonel punched the buzzer and waited. A couple of seconds later his identity was verified by Captain Sara Chavez, who opened the vault door. She was an attractive woman, her dark hair tied to the back of her head. Although she wore camouflage fatigues, it was quite apparent that she kept herself fit with running, which had become more difficult, the colonel thought, considering the limited distances on Shemya Island. Not to mention the ubiquitous wind and rain. The treadmill had to do the job in the winter.

"Morning, Sir," she said, stepping aside.

"Morning, Sara. How's the coffee."

"A bit strong," she said, closing the vault door behind him.

Before even checking the status board, the colonel poured himself a cup of thick, black coffee. Then he glanced about the small compartment. Besides Captain Chavez, there was one other command controller present; Staff Sergeant Greg Wilson, who sat at a console with headphones.

The colonel took his chair in the back overlooking the status boards and control panels. Most of the panels were inoperative now, phased out by more sophisticated communications, centralized in Colorado. However, the colonel had insisted that they have the most recent communications upgraded as soon as possible, and some of that had already come online.

Captain Chavez stood to the colonel's side, sipping her coffee.

The colonel took a sip and his face crunched. "Wow, Sara. Is this a west Texas brew?"

She smiled. "Damn straight. Put hair on your chest."

"More like curl the hair on your chest," he said. "Where's our plane?"

She turned to Sergeant Wilson. “Greg?”

“Twenty miles out,” the sergeant said. “They reported some heavy head winds. You want me to patch you through?”

“That’s all right, Greg. Let ‘em fly.”

Colonel Powers drank some more coffee and then turned to the captain again. “We have security police on the tarmac standing by?”

“Yes, Sir,” she said. Bravo Flight.”

“Outstanding.”

“Yes, Sir. Out standing in the cold.” She smiled.

Finally, the colonel laughed. “How long have you waited for that?”

“Just came to me, Sir.”

“What else we got on that plane, Sara?”

She picked up a clipboard and flipped to the second page. “A Master Sergeant Jones and Senior Airman Cato. Both are programmers.”

“That’s Jonesy!” he said. “We worked together in Germany. Best point guard we ever had on our basketball team. I don’t know Cato. What else?”

“Looks like some fresh salmon again.”

“Great! Just what we need. . .more fish.”

The colonel sucked down the last of his coffee and got up for more. When he turned around, the captain was leaning over the console talking with Sergeant Wilson, her buttocks pointing right in his direction. Damn! He shook it off and took a seat again.

There were five monitors that sequenced through various security cameras placed around the base. From the commander’s chair, the colonel could switch to whichever view he wanted and keep it there while the others continued to sequence. He toggled to the corridor above and saw the two security police reading magazines. Then he went to an outside view. Nice job on the sidewalk, he thought. Next he went to the control tower and saw the C-130 had just landed and was now rolling slowly to a halt in front of the operations building. So he switched to the camera above operations and waited.

“The plane has landed,” the captain said, turning around, and realizing he was watching the monitor. “But you know that.” She stood next to the commander’s chair and watched with him.

The ground crew pushed a ladder to the plane and then the door opened. Standing back a ways was Bravo Flight with at least fifteen security police airmen. On the perimeter was a Humvee with an M60 machine gun mounted on top and manned. The others had M16s and were spread out around the plane.

The next few seconds were chaos. One of the men getting off the plane fell to the ground. But the security police turned away, reacting to something else.

"What's going on?" the colonel yelled.

Sergeant Wilson held his hand to his headphone. "Sir, there's gunfire."

"What?"

They watched in horror as a second man fell.

Then the security police returned fire in a burst and took up secure positions behind their Humvees.

CHAPTER 19

Jake and Su had slept most of the day, knowing they would be up much of the night traveling through the mountains. He was certain Su's uncle had no idea why they were there, which was a good thing, since Jake was beginning to wonder himself.

Jake was offered a mix of winter clothes that the uncle kept around for when his relatives happened by in the colder months. Judging from their tattered state, they were probably as old as Su. The green wool pants seemed to be from Mao's military and were a snug fit on him. His biggest concern, though, were the mukluks, which Su explained were made mostly of yak hide and fur, but were very tight on his larger feet. He wasn't complaining, though. All of the items were made with dull colors and would keep him warm. Better yet, they might have made him stick out less, especially when he wore the thick fur hat that covered much of his face.

Su had told her uncle that Jake was a winter survivalist, and China, and particularly Manchuria, was on his list of experiences he must accomplish before the age of fifty. The uncle had laughed at that, shaking his head as he smiled. Crazy Americans.

Now, with the sun slowly creeping toward the western mountains, Jake and Su stood on a path at the end of a narrow road. Her uncle had just dropped them off with his little truck, still scratching his head like the two of them were complete idiots as he drove off in a plume of smoke toward town.

"So," Jake said, "I guess your uncle must think you're nuts."

She slung her large backpack over her shoulders, and when she got it caught on her heavy coat, Jake helped her put it in place on her back.

"Thanks. Really, he only thinks you're crazy. I told him you paid me one thousand American to guide you here." She smiled broadly with that revelation. "You ready?"

"You're a funny woman. Yeah, let's go." He put on his own pack and trudged off.

The snow was only about a foot deep. Nothing compared to what he was used to in the Austrian Alps, but the cold, dry wind nearly took his breath away. They first cleared a small field and then started heading up in elevation. The trail was perhaps ten feet wide and soon started to wind through a thick, fir forest.

Jake stopped and turned to Su. "Is this a road?"

She reached him and halted a moment. "Kind of. In the summer the villagers lead their livestock up to high meadows to eat grass. My uncle uses the road to cut wood for his stove and fireplace. Please, Jake, we must keep moving."

Without a word, Jake headed out again. After a couple of miles, they reached a ridge that flattened out and appeared to rise up slightly to the west and to the north. There was a small meadow where the snow was deeper.

Su stopped and scanned the area, uncertain. The sun was nearly history and the temperature would soon start to drop fast.

"What's the matter?" Jake asked.

"Nothing. We're about half way." She pointed off toward the north. "You see. We walk parallel to the road some four miles north, but the road comes this way some. So, we catch up on the plateau."

"I take it there's no trail now?" Jake said.

"That's right." With that, she stepped off into the deeper snow and into the thickest of trees.

With the coming darkness and the tight forest, the canopy above them let in very little light. But there was one advantage to that. The dense fir trees had let much less snow hit the ground. They would have been able to pick up their pace if it had not been for the darkness.

His mind drifted back to America and Oregon in particular. In college he had climbed through the coast range after a heavy snowfall, the trees thick and heavy with the weight of snow. Although the forest cover was similar, the cold was not. His nostrils seemed to collapse with each breath he took. Perhaps a bigger problem, though, was his perspiration soaking into his clothes. He knew that when he stopped hiking, the wet, damp wool would freeze and drop his core temperature. They had extra clothes in the backpacks to reduce that eventuality, but that extra weight also compounded the problem. It was like hiking in the desert. The more water you carried the more water you needed.

Jake noticed Su was starting to slump over slightly. "Su, maybe we should change packs," he said. "Yours must weigh fifty pounds."

She didn't stop, though. She straightened up and said, "I'm all right."

Once it was almost impossible to see in front of them, Su pulled out a small pen light and strapped it to the side of her backpack.

Still, the going was slow. At that pace, Jake thought, they would reach their destination around midnight. Perfect timing, but their exhaustion might have a negative impact on their mission there.

Nevertheless, they trudged on through the cold, dark forest.

CHAPTER 20

They were at a standoff. Cliff sat on his friend's sofa, and Patterson was in his recliner, his legs raised and his hands behind his head. Li sat on the floor, legs crossed, a laptop computer in front of her and her gun no more than a few inches from her right hand.

"I didn't know you had a laptop," Cliff said to her.

"Shut up! You asshole." The words came out like that of a child first learning them. Stilted. Unsure.

Both Cliff and Patterson laughed, which made Li raise her gun, not even looking in their direction. They both stopped immediately.

"Listen," Cliff said, his hands pleading. "I can't give you the encryption code until you give me the money. That's the deal."

"The deal changed," she said. "You got the money."

"What money?" Patterson said, hunching his broad shoulders. "What the hell you guys talkin' about?"

"Shut fuck up!" Li yelled at him, which brought another chuckle from both men. "You won't laugh soon," she assured them. Then she pointed the gun at Cliff's head. "The codes!"

"I need the money," Cliff pleaded. "It's not like I can ever go back to Brightstar. But I would like to go someplace warm."

"How 'bout Hell," she said, smiling. "I hear it's warm there always."

"Fuckin' A. This is going nowhere. I thought we cut a deal. Now you're yankin' me around."

"You yank me around," she said. "Drive all over the damn country when you could have sent it to your house in the Bay Area. That's bull-shit and you know it."

"They woulda traced that in a heartbeat. No shit."

Neither said a word for a moment, but she did lower her gun while she punched in a few more key strokes on the laptop. Cliff glanced at his friend, who didn't seem too concerned.

Finally, Li picked up her cell phone and speed dialed a number. Then she rattled off some Chinese, shook her head as she looked at the two men, and clicked off by flipping the phone shut.

"I give you one more chance to give me encryption codes," she said to Cliff. She raised the gun again.

Cliff leaned forward in the chair. "I can't. I need the money. You agreed on a mil."

She let out a sigh, swiveled the gun to her left, and shot twice. The first bullet hit Patterson in the middle of his chest, the shock knocking him back in his recliner. The second shot became a red spot on his forehead.

Cliff rose to his feet. "What the fuck!" he yelled. His eyes were wide with horror. "You killed him." His breathing increased, his heart pounding out of control. Finally, tears came to his eyes and he sobbed uncontrollably.

Li got up from the floor and pointed the gun at Cliff now. "You need to focus, Cliff. Your life is worth a split second. That's all it takes to pull a trigger."

He turned to her, his eyes red and tears streaking his face. "You didn't have to do that, Li. I was gonna give ya the codes. I just...I just wanted some more time with you. That's all. Ya didn't have to do this." He pointed at his friend in the recliner, where blood had now escaped from his chest and was running down the sides to the floor.

"I warn you, Cliff. The codes."

"There are no codes," he yelled. "It's an encryption scheme built into a program I developed. A five-twelve scheme. Do you know what that is?"

"I know one thing," she started, "your friend died for about a buck. I love America. Cheap bullets. Pow pow. Less than a buck. Crazy how life is so cheap."

"You're fuckin' nuts, bitch."

"The codes."

"I'm telling you there are no codes. I encrypted the entire file with a five-twelve scheme. You and your pal on the phone could try for a million years and never break that scheme." He wiped his tears away and smiled.

She considered what he had just said, uncertain. She pulled out the phone and made another call. This time her voice seemed more desperate. She finally let out a deep breath and hung up.

"Give me the encryption program," she said.

He swiveled his head from side to side. "I do that and you kill me. You give me the money. Once that clears, then I send you the program remotely. But not until I'm out of the range of that." He pointed at her gun.

"You know. If I want, I could hunt you down like a dog and kill you. Even after you give me the program."

"I believe you, Li." He glanced over at his old college friend.

Finally, she said, "All right. Let's go to the bank."

♦

The two Network officers, Harris and Fisher, were sitting in their chairs in the white Ford Taurus, less than a block from Patterson's house. Fisher was behind the wheel trying his best to see through the rain-streaked windshield, keeping his eyes on the Trooper, and Harris was switching channels on the radio attempting to find a station that would give her a decent weather report.

"This is bullshit!" Harris said.

"They're used to this crap," Fisher said to her. "Don't need no stinkin' weather report in Eugene. It's gonna rain until it stops. Wait a minute. Got something here."

They watched as the Asian woman and Cliff Johansen exited the house and shuffled toward the Trooper.

Agent Harris buckled her seat belt. "Looks like we're rolling."

Fisher thought as he started the engine and desperately fought to clear the foggy windshield. "You wouldn't happen to know where the closest branch of the Bank of the Pacific is located."

Harris shook her head.

"Same here. But I think we're about to find out."

He pulled out after the Trooper, which was now rolling through the quiet neighborhood toward the Willamette River.

CHAPTER 21

Arlington, Virginia

Darkness was starting to settle on the capitol across the Potomac as the lone, black Mercedes pulled up to the curb at the small park two blocks from the George Washington Memorial Parkway.

Stepping out to the pavement, Karl Oestreich, dressed in his finest gray suit, having come right from the White House, closed the door behind him and locked it electronically.

General Wayne Boles stood fifty yards up a small hill and barely acknowledged the Chief of Staff's arrival. His arms hung behind his back in a near parade rest. Unlike his old friend, he wore khaki pants and a Washington Redskins windbreaker.

"This better be good," Oestreich said as he made his way up the hill.

When the Chief of Staff reached the retired general, Boles finally said, "Why don't you make a little more noise? I don't think they heard you over in Georgetown."

"Hey, this cloak and dagger shit was your idea," Oestreich said. "What's up?"

Boles shifted his head about as a jogger passed on the road below. "Our man in China."

"Adams?"

"Right. He hasn't made contact since leaving Beijing."

Oestreich laughed under his breath. "I thought he was an obstinate bastard. Shouldn't come as a surprise to you."

"Yeah, but there was a problem with one of our agents in Harbin."

"Where the fuck is that?"

"Manchuria...Northern China," Boles said. "The Network recruited him out of Stanford."

"So, what's the problem?"

Boles hesitated. "He got himself killed."

"Great. Any fallout on our end?"

The general shook his head. "But we got reports that the police are after a Chinese woman accompanied by an American man. They were seen leaving the scene."

Oestreich turned and looked across the Potomac as the last light faded from the Washington Memorial. "Sounds like a typical Chinese set up to me. Kill the contact and grab the patsy who shows up next. I take it the woman is working for us as well?"

"Yeah. Also recruited from Stanford. The three of them were to drive north to the site."

"Call them off!"

"But..."

"Just do it," the Chief of Staff said. "Their mission must have been compromised. Let me guess. The agent was tortured."

Boles didn't say a word.

"Then Adams is probably fucked."

"Karl, we need this info. We can't afford to pull him."

The Chief of Staff thought about it. "Adams is good. But what if that dead agent said where they were heading? They'd be waiting for him to show his face. And, having seen satellite shots of that region, Adams will stick out like a black man in Alaska. Which reminds me...we got a problem there as well."

"I heard. Lone gunman?"

"Still not sure. The air force security police filled him so full of lead he's likely to be the next Superfund site."

Boles laughed. "Anybody ever tell you you're a master of overstatement?"

"Just my fuckin' liberal lesbian sister. How we gonna help Adams in Manchuria?"

"I'm working on it," Boles said, smiling and raising his brows.

"Is this one of those plausible deniability scenarios? Better I don't know all the details?"

Hunching his shoulders, Boles said, "The Network in China is wrapped tighter than a Baptist virgin. Let us handle it."

"Good. I got a dinner party."

"Over at the Hilton?"

Oestreich turned to Boles. "Christ you got my entire schedule?"

"Someone's gotta keep track of our public officials."

The Chief of Staff laughed as he walked down the hill.

The general waited for the Mercedes to pull away and then retrieved his cell phone from his pocket and punched in the long number overseas.

When a man finally answered, he said, "Do it." Then he flipped his phone shut and glanced across the Potomac at the buildings of power. They had a saying in the Air Force. 'Whatever it takes.' They were words he lived by even now.

CHAPTER 22

The trek through the snowy mountains had become even more difficult as Jake and Su had gotten closer to the Chinese military site. They had been forced to turn off their light, and, since they didn't have night vision equipment, they had to rely on the occasional flicker of moon through swirling clouds to guide them for a few unencumbered steps. Needless to say, the going had been slow.

They had pulled a thin winter camo shell from Su's backpack and stretched it over their other clothes, cinching ties at their ankles and wrists, the white, gray and green shades allowing them to blend into their surroundings. This wouldn't help much in the darkness, but once it got light again, they would be almost impossible to spot among the trees. The camo would do nothing, however, should the Chinese military use infrared binoculars, Jake knew.

Now they sat, exhausted, on a precipice among thick firs overlooking an enormous compound that Jake was sure would show up on satellite photos. But what would they see? There was a large dome that, by every stretch of the imagination, would appear as a huge telescope. The largest building resembled a monastic temple. There were at least a half a dozen other buildings with snow-covered roofs, that, from the air, would appear to be nothing more than barracks or dormitories, depending on the interpretation of the analyst. Glancing around the entire compound, which was not enclosed by a tall fence with razor wire, or any fence at all that he could see, Jake noticed all of the vehicles were civilian. In fact, those walking from building to building wore clothes much like those he had gotten from Su's uncle. No military uniforms at all.

"Are we at the right place?" Jake asked Su softly.

She nodded her head.

"I don't see any military here? There are no weapons."

"There's one road in," she said. "I would guess there's a check-point at least a mile down the mountain. It would look like a Hutong from the air. Nothing more. But they would stop anyone wanting to go up the mountain. Not that anyone would want to."

"Why not?"

"They think the people are stupid," she said, her eyes still focused on the compound below. "They see the military arrive in the village by train. Then there are no more military in town. Where do they go each day?"

Jake smiled. "They change into civilian clothes and come up here. But why all the secrecy?"

"That's why we're here," Su said.

That got Jake thinking. And he should have kicked himself for not thinking of it sooner. He opened his backpack and pulled out the digital camera that the Think Tank man, Steve Anderson, had given him. The camera had an infra-red feature. He could take a photo in the darkness, without flash, and then view it on the back. Although he wouldn't be able to see much through the lens, he hoped the viewer would reveal something.

After messing with the buttons to make sure the flash would not go off and reveal their position, Jake aimed the camera and took a shot.

"I've never seen a camera like that," Su said. "What does it do?"

Instead of answering, Jake shifted closer to her and showed her the image in the back of the camera. He had taken a shot of the dome in high quality setting.

"Wow. That's nice."

Jake had to agree. The image looked almost like day.

Then Jake got another idea. He dug down into his bag and pulled out the phone.

"Damn," Jake said.

"What?"

"I was supposed to call in once we left Harbin with your friend."

As he mentioned her dead college friend, her eyes seemed to sadden, as if she had just found out about his death for the first time.

Jake focused and retrieved a cord that would connect the camera to the phone. He turned on the phone, which was supposed to work anywhere in China, but he got no signal.

"Dead spot?" she asked. "But it should work. We put up a tower ten miles to the south last fall." Then she thought about it and took out her phone and tried it. "Nothing. This is crazy."

"Maybe the signal is being jammed somehow," Jake said. "Would it be hard to do it?"

"Not easy. Not hard."

"Is this one of those Yin and Yang things?"

"Maybe."

Jake put the phone back and started shooting a few more shots.

"How many can you take with that?" she asked him.

"Depends on the quality. At this distance we want the highest we can get so they can blow it up." He glanced at her and could barely see her eyes in the darkness. "We have to get closer."

"We can't. Not without three. My friend was our in. We can't just walk in."

"Why not? There are no fences. No guards." Jake didn't believe his own words; he was just trying to test her knowledge and resolve.

"What is not there is not always seen. What is seen is not always there."

"Sounds like a Taoist conundrum to me," Jake said.

Her eyes looked hurt, as if he had just insulted her.

"That was a joke," Jake assured her.

"I don't get it."

Jake didn't have time to explain himself.

Suddenly, the domed observatory came to life. First, there was the 180 degree twist. Then the top of the dome opened. Not like a normal observatory, with just enough room for the large telescope to swivel across the sky, but this dome retracted back like an eyelid opening from a deep sleep.

Jake took a couple of shots.

Next, something rose up from inside the observatory. It looked almost like an industrial robot that would spot-weld cars on an assembly line.

One more shot.

The robot-like contraption adjusted back and forth, as if it was confused.

By the time Jake or Su knew what they were hearing, it was over. Jake had continued shooting shots one after the next. But he wasn't sure what he was shooting. Nor was he sure what was happening in the compound below.

And then, as if a magician was finally revealing his trick, things became more clear to Jake.

High above, the clouds had opened for just a moment. Just long enough for Jake to see the object crossing the sky.

Then came the explosion. And Jake got the shot.

"What just happened?" Su asked him.

Jake didn't answer right away. Maybe he wasn't entirely certain himself. However, seeing the dome on the observatory cover the robot object again, he was more certain.

"That, my friend, was a near miss by a ground-based laser on a flying object at about twenty thousand feet."

"But it blew up."

"That's right. But there was too much delay. From the time they powered up the laser to the explosion was too long. It should have happened much sooner. That was an abort. Self destruct. Did you see how the laser jerked about trying to acquire the target?"

"Yeah."

"That's a software problem," he said. "Looks like they have the laser working, but they still can't tell it what to do."

"I don't understand. I thought we were just verifying a missile site that could strike the U.S. west coast."

Damn. They had really kept her in the dark, Jake thought.

"What does this mean?" she continued.

There wasn't time to answer her. Without warning, the compound below was full of activity. Soldiers in civilian clothes ran about. Then one pointed in their direction.

"Shit!" Jake said, grabbing her arm. "Let's go."

Slinging their backpacks on, they ran in the direction from which they had come. How had they known? Jake had no idea. They must have had a broad array of motion sensors. How was not important, he knew. All that mattered was his reaction.

He smashed his way through the trees, and he could feel Su right on his heels.

CHAPTER 23

Beijing

They were only to meet on the north shore of Yuyuan Lake if something serious had happened.

Special Agent Brian Armstrong had called his contact, Steve Anderson, from the conservative think tank, and simply said, “Time for a swim.” Then he had hung up.

In the darkness on the lake shore, Armstrong leaned against a large oak. During the day, he thought, the place was one of the most pleasant parks in Beijing. But at night it was a different story. Darkness shrouded the entire shoreline and cast shadows outward to the lake from the surrounding buildings, which were low and dark, but for a few lights. If he looked carefully, now that his eyes had adjusted, Armstrong could see movement. A man? He pushed himself closer to the tree. He had only a butterfly knife in his pocket, which he ran through the fingers on his right hand.

He tried his best to control his breathing, but he feared he was failing miserably. He wanted to pull out his inhaler and take a shot, but the shadow was too close.

Then he felt a hand touch him.

“That water has to be cold,” his contact said quietly.

“Not as cold as the air,” Armstrong answered. “You’re late.”

“I was in the hot tub.”

“Must be nice.”

“I can’t wait to get back. What’s up?”

Armstrong looked about, not seeing or hearing anything unusual. “There was an explosion up north. We think it was a test.”

"Damn. Was it successful?"

"We don't know."

"Any word from our man up there?"

"That's why I'm here," Armstrong said, trying his best not to get outwardly disturbed. "He should have contacted you by now. You haven't heard a thing?"

"I would have told you," Anderson assured him defiantly. "What's goin' on here?"

Armstrong let out a deep breath and almost coughed. Then he finally pulled out his inhaler and took a long draw on it. Almost instantly he could breath again.

"Our man in Harbin is dead," Armstrong forced out.

"Adams is dead?"

"No. Our Chinese contact. The programmer from Stanford." Armstrong was getting disturbed now, wondering if Anderson had lost his mind.

"How?"

"Beaten to death. Cut. Tortured."

"What about Adams and the girl?"

"Got away. But no word. The police are after them, I'm sure."

"We've gotta pull Adams," Anderson said. "He's compromised."

"We don't know that. He could be in the mountains right now. Besides, we have no way of pulling him."

Anderson laughed. "GPS."

"What?"

"He can be tracked by a GPS transceiver we planted in the backpack handle."

"And you didn't tell us?"

"Need to know."

"I needed to know."

"Now you do."

There was a slight noise off behind the both of them, some fifty feet away. An animal maybe.

"Here," Anderson said, passing the Network officer a piece of paper, which he would have to wait to read. "The GPS code to locate Adams. As I'm sure you know, turn it on only for a couple of seconds at a time. The signal goes both ways. The Chinese could pick up on it without too much trouble."

"Thanks," Armstrong breathed heavily.

"No problem. Can I get back to my hot tub now?"

"Yeah."

With that, Anderson patted the Network man on his arm and headed off into the darkness.

Armstrong waited a few seconds and then started off. Then he heard it. A struggle? A release of air?

In the shroud of black, Armstrong shuffled toward the noise. Then, without warning, he tumbled over something and landed on his hands, then his face. He shook his head and moved his hands about the icy ground. His right hand touched something. A leg? His hand reached up until it settled on a warm, wet, sticky substance. Blood. Damn it! He wiped his hand on the frozen ground, and then scooted toward the person's head.

"Steve," he whispered, and then tilted his head toward the man's face.

But there was no sound that would come from him again. All he heard was a gurgling of frothy blood from the man's lungs. He checked for a carotid pulse. Nothing.

Then it kicked in. The adrenaline of fear. He could be next. He scanned the entire area around him, but he could see nothing more than shadows. He pulled out his butterfly knife and flipped it open with ease. He tried to use distant lights as a reference point. Anybody who crossed them and he would at least see the silhouette.

There! A figure moved swiftly across his view.

Armstrong took chase. He kept low, the lights out in front of him.

Soon he reached Fucheng Road, which was deserted at this late hour. Across and skirting into an alley, he saw the figure again.

At first he wasn't sure what was happening to him. He felt his heart trying to escape through his mouth, which was wide open and struggling for each new breath. His head got lighter and his knees buckled.

Seconds later he was on his butt in the frozen grass alongside the road, one hand clutching his knife and the other rifling through his pocket for his inhaler. Finally he found it and took a long shot into his mouth.

Then came the sirens heading in his direction.

He looked down at his bloody hand and his butterfly knife and realized he had to get the hell out of there.

Pulling himself to his feet, he shuffled across the road toward his car.

CHAPTER 24

Eugene, Oregon

The rain had slowed some, but the sun was nowhere in sight. Cliff Johansen was like a trapped animal. He knew that Li had her gun ready with one swift motion, and he also knew she was willing to use it. My God, he thought, she had just killed his old college buddy as if he were a bug. No emotions. No regret. Would she do the same to him? Especially once she got what she needed?

They sat in the white Trooper now in the parking lot of the downtown branch of the Bank of the Pacific. He was numb.

"Just like last time," Li said. "We transfer the money and you get the program from your safe deposit box. I will shoot you." She left it at that.

He was sweating now. He rubbed the palms of his hands together and then wiped them on his pants. "Why'd you have to kill Jimmy?"

"I don't have to do anything but return with this DVD and a way to access the files." She tapped the DVD in the side pocket of her leather coat. Then she looked down and noticed something. "Damn. Rain fucked up my leather. Should make you buy me a new one."

"I'll send you the money with the encryption scheme," Cliff said.

"Enough bullshit," she said. "The bank will close in half hour. Let's go!"

The two of them got out and shuffled through the parking lot toward the back door. Once inside, Cliff stopped and looked around.

"What wrong?" she asked. "This your bank. You should know where everything at." She grabbed his arm and squeezed at a spot behind his biceps.

He cringed. "It's been a while, all right?" He nodded his head and they walked to a young woman at a desk.

♦

Just behind Cliff and the Asian woman, Special Agent Harris made her way to a center stand and started filling out a withdrawal form. Then she patted her pockets and started searching her purse, her eyes trying to keep from making full contact with her two subjects behind her.

She pulled out her cell phone and punched in a number. Two rings later, Agent Fisher answered in the car outside.

"Honey, I forgot the savings book," she said.

When she got a nasty look from the woman across from her, she made a sorry gesture and then turned her back, lowering her voice. Now she could watch Cliff and the Asian woman.

"You call me Honey again and I might shoot you," Fisher said on the other end of the phone. "So, what are they up to this time?"

She whispered now. "Sitting down with a bank official. Looks like another electronic transfer." Then she said more loudly, "It might be on the kitchen counter." She glanced back, her hand on the phone, and said to the woman, "Sorry. Thank God the sex is great."

The woman smiled and went to the next teller.

"I heard that," Fisher said. "And how'd you know?"

"Focus, Dear. Our man just got up to go somewhere with the banker. The woman is looking right at me. Better go." Then she said louder, "Thanks, Honey. You saved me."

She flipped the phone shut and turned back to the table to fill out her form.

♦

In the vault, Cliff kept looking back to see if Li had followed them.

The young bank official, who looked no more than twenty-five, had a concerned expression on her face. "Is everything all right, Mr. Johansen?"

He turned to her. "Yes. I'm sorry. No. No, everything is not all right."

"You can get a larger size for only thirty dollars more a year," she said. "Would that be better?"

He moved toward the vault door, glanced back, and then turned to her.

"Is there some sort of panic button back here? An alarm?"

Now the young woman was afraid. "You don't have a gun, do you? I've only worked here a month."

"No. I don't," he said. "But my friend out there does. And she'll kill us both if she knows I'm even discussing this with you."

She was silent, biting her upper lip. "But she just transferred five hundred thousand into your account. Why would she be trying to rob the bank?"

Cliff shook his head. "You don't understand. She's not trying to rob you. She wants something from me. If I give it to her she might not kill me. If I don't give it to her, she will kill me. But she might just kill me for the hell of it no matter what I do. Do you understand?"

Her eyes shifted toward the door. "So, you want the cops to show up and arrest her?"

"That would help," he said to her, "but then I might be in more trouble."

"The half a million."

"Right. That's part of it. What should I do?"

She shook her head. "You're asking me? I dropped out of college last year. I...I don't know."

Cliff thought hard, sweat dripping from his forehead. He was stuck. If he went with her, she'd kill him either way, he was sure of that. If he called the cops in on her, one of her associates would come after him. Maybe he should just give her the encryption scheme here in the bank. Then he could refuse to leave. Being in public, she couldn't pull the gun on him. It might work. He checked his watch.

"You close in fifteen minutes?"

She nodded her head. "A lot of people get paid on Fridays and they want us open later."

"All right," he said. "Here's what I want you to do." He explained his plan to her, hoping she wouldn't freeze when he needed her. Then the two of them headed out into the lobby.

Cliff took a seat next to Li. He smiled at her and said, "All right. Got it. You go to your laptop in the Trooper. I'll call you on your cell phone and tell you how to open the files."

"You come with me."

"No. I do that and you kill me."

"I kill you right here." She slid her hand inside her jacket.

"I wouldn't. Look at our young helper at the counter."

When the two of them looked at the young banker, she gave two thumbs up.

"If you don't leave by yourself, she hits the alarm and this entire block will be locked down with cops faster than you can say Chop Suey."

She shook her head. "That's Japanese."

"Whatever. You get the point."

"Give me the encryption codes," she said, her voice determined.

Cliff hesitated, unsure what to do or how far to push her. She would kill him, he was sure of that much. Finally, he said, "The encryption scheme is on the DVD. Open it when prompted with the password 'Felatio.'"

"You wish. I will check it on my laptop. It doesn't open and I shoot you."

He shrugged his shoulders.

She got up from her chair, leaned down toward him, and gave him a kiss on the cheek. "I faked all orgasms with you," she whispered. "Your penis is too small." She smiled and started to leave. Then she put her arm around his neck and spoke softly into his ear. "You cross me and I kill anyone you ever know. Understand?"

He smiled at her. "Nice doin' business with you."

She left him there, his face sweating as if he had just run a marathon.

CHAPTER 25

They had nowhere to go. Yet, Jake and Su were on the run back the same way they had come across the ridge, following their own tracks through the snow. But that was futile, Jake knew. Eventually they would be caught.

When they came across a small stream that was open from hot springs, Jake stopped Su by grabbing her arm.

"We can't do this," Jake said, out of breath. "This way!" He pulled her down the narrow stream.

Running as carefully as possible through the darkness and unsure footing, they soon came to a small waterfall. They would have to cross around the outside on tall rocks.

Although it was quite dark, there was an occasional break where the moon would poke out from behind clouds, and the wind seemed to pick up with each step they took down the mountain.

They skirted around the rocks, which were icy and wet near the falls, and then Su lost her footing. As she started to fall, Jake grabbed her hand and the two of them, with heavy backpacks, hurtled down the rocks.

It was not a huge drop to the first time they hit, but then they continued to roll, bouncing off rocks and crashing through the small trees between them, until they hit an opening. Then they started to slide down the embankment of snow, sliding through trees whipping them in their face, until their final plunge into the icy water.

If the water had been deeper, they might have ended up at the bottom of the river, never to rise again. But the small pool they hit was only a couple of feet deep.

Jake struggled to his feet, disoriented. He saw Su face down in the pool.

He slung her around and dragged her to the embankment. He gave her mouth-to-mouth until she released some water and started coughing.

Pulling out a pen light, he looked her over for injuries. She had a few scratches on her face, but nothing serious. He moved his hands over her body, trying to check for broken bones.

Her breathing improved and she shook her head. "Usually I demand dinner before we get to this point," she said.

"Very funny. Any pain?"

"How about a loss of dignity?" She sat up, struggling against the backpack.

"That only counts if one falls and not the other." He ran his hands down each arm until he got to her left wrist.

"Oww."

Slowly, Jake worked her sleeve up and saw the black and blue and the swelling.

"Broken?" she asked.

"Afraid so." He put her sleeve down. Then he glanced up the mountain. "We've gotta get going."

He pulled her to her feet and then they both realized the real problem. They were wet from the waist up, and the backpacks had taken on water, which made them heavier. Worse yet, the cold wind would have them lose heat as fast as their bodies produced it.

Together they worked their way down the mountain stream, which gained width with their progress. The only thing that saved them from hypothermia was their constant movement.

Once the river hit a small step, they stopped to catch their breath.

"I don't hear them behind us," Su said, her breathing labored and her good hand gently rubbing the broken wrist.

Jake didn't answer. Instead, he pulled out the light and dug into his backpack. He found his phone and tried to pick up a signal.

Nothing.

"Damn it!" he said.

Su gasped, her eyes wide as she stared at Jake.

"What?"

She said something in Chinese as she moved closer, her good hand moving to the left side of Jake's face. "You have a huge gash here," she said.

He pulled off his gloves and felt at his head, finding crusted blood and eventually a raised area at his left temple, which was still sticky with oozing blood. He winced in pain as he touched the cut area.

"Great."

Digging into his backpack he found a small Ziploc bag with a few items inside. It held small bandages, band-aids and tape. But first he needed something else. There. He found a small tube of super glue.

"Could you help me?" he asked her. "Squeeze some of this on the wound."

"That's glue," she protested.

"Just do it!"

She shrugged and then did what he asked with her good hand. "You crazy."

Next he pulled out a couple of butterfly bandages and had her pull the wound together.

"That should work," he said, putting everything back into his pack. "Let's go."

"I don't think they're following us," she said.

"Maybe not. But it doesn't matter. If we don't get out of these clothes, we'll be stiff as a board by morning."

She agreed with her silent nod.

They moved downstream a little slower now, spending more time on the bank than in the water.

Although his clothes were heavy with the stream water, Jake still had not caught a chill. Perhaps it was the constant movement. Maybe it was the clothes he had gotten from Su's uncle. Either way, he was thankful for that one luxury. Now if only he could get the information, the photos he had taken, uploaded on the cell phone. That might have to wait until they reached the valley. Something in the mountains was blocking the signal.

After a while the terrain started to get less steep, and the river changed from a gurgling churn to a wider ripple. He checked his watch. The sun would be starting to come up within an hour or so.

But one question kept seeping up to the front of his mind. Why had the soldiers stopped following them?

He got his answer in a few minutes, and it made Jake and Su stop dead in their tracks alongside the river.

The familiar sound of a helicopter rose up from the valley below.

Now came the chill.

CHAPTER 26

By the time Cliff Johansen felt safe to exit the bank, his breathing had finally started to get back to normal. Instead of going out the back door to the parking lot, he exited the front door to the downtown sidewalk.

Just as he reached the sidewalk, a hand grasped his neck and shoved him forward against a brown Ford Taurus.

Instinctively, his hands caught his fall on the top of the car.

"Get in," came a harsh woman's voice.

He tried to turn around, when an elbow smashed him in the mouth, disorienting him and bringing tears to his eyes.

All he remembered next was being shoved into the back seat, a person jumping in next to him, and the car pulling away from the curb.

"You got her?" the woman's voice asked the driver.

"Three blocks up she took a left," the man said.

Cliff rubbed the tears from his eyes and then tried to stop his bleeding lip. He shook his head to get his vision.

"Take my money," Cliff said. "I don't have much, though."

The woman laughed. "You gotta be the dumbest mother fucker in Oregon."

Cliff shrugged. "What?"

"Like we really want cash from you." She considered pulling out her I.D. and flashing it in his face, but then thought of something better. "We would like the final account where you just sent that half a million bucks."

Cliff's eyes shot up at her, confused. "What million bucks?"

"Now, Cliff," she said.

The car careened through the intersection, turning sharply left, sliding Cliff into Agent Harris.

She continued, "I said half a million."

"Oh..."

"I hadn't even included the half a million you transferred this morning in Bend. But now that you brought it up, let's find out about that as well."

He sunk into his seat. "Who the hell are you?"

"Eugene cops got her out on I-5 heading north," the driver said. "They're holding back, waiting for us to catch up."

The car rounded the on ramp to the interstate and picked up speed.

Suddenly, there was a light that seemed to go on in Cliff's brain. He was sitting right behind the driver, so he couldn't see the man's face.

"What's the matter, Cliff?" she asked. "You don't look great. That's what betraying your country will do to you."

His head shot toward her. "What the fuck. You can't."

"Can't what, Cliff? Prove that you took secret technology from Brightstar and took a payoff from the Asian woman driving in the white Trooper about a half mile ahead? That's treason, my man. You'll never see that money. Better yet, you'll end up at the other end of a needle. Which, in my opinion, is too good for you. I was hoping you'd try to escape so I can shoot your ass." She started reaching for her gun.

"Who the fuck are you?" Cliff yelled.

Agent Fisher turned his head to the back seat for an instant and then back to the highway. "A little more intense than life behind the cubicle, hey Cliff?"

"Steve? Steve Lempi?" Cliff said. "What the. . ?"

"Actually," the driver said, "you might want to start calling me by my real name, Drew Fisher. I'm with the Network."

"A journalist?" Cliff asked, confused.

"No, you dumb fuck. The Network." He emphasized both words.

Harris shook her head. "I thought you said he was a brilliant programmer?"

Fisher shrugged his shoulders.

"Wait a minute," Cliff said. "You worked in Group Five."

"Yeah," Fisher said. "And my mother was the Tooth Fairy."

"She was!" Harris said.

"You know what I mean."

The light bulb got brighter in Cliff's brain. "Shit!"

"Don't get too close," Harris said, tapping her hand on the driver's seat.

"I'll tell you what," Fisher said. "I'll drive and you take care of Butthead."

"Deal." She swung her left hand, catching Cliff in the forehead and knocking him back against the seat.

When Cliff recovered, he said, "What the hell was that for?"

"That's for the next lie that comes out of your mouth. I just wanted to get ahead of the game."

"You're a sick bitch."

She went to hit him and he jerked his head back, bashing it against the side window.

"Hey," Fisher said. "We might need him to testify."

"I didn't do that," she pleaded.

"Sure."

The car stayed back, leaving a large pickup truck blocking their view of the Trooper a few cars up the road.

"Where's she going, Cliff?" Harris asked him.

"How should I know?" He put his hands in front of his face and then peered out between his fingers before lowering his guard.

"You are the worst liar," she said. Then her phone rang and she pulled it from her inside pocket and simply said, "Harris."

She listened carefully, and then said, "How long?" Pause. "We've got him right here." Her eyes considered Cliff more seriously. "Thanks." She slowly flipped the phone shut and returned it to her pocket.

"Who was that?" Fisher asked.

She hesitated and then said, "Portland. It seems our man here is now an accessory to murder."

Cliff pulled forward against his seat belt. "I had nothing to do with killin' Jimmy."

Now she was confused. "Did I say Jimmy?"

"She killed him for no reason," Cliff said, tears growing in his eyes again. "Shot him for no reason. Bam.

Bam."

"Shit!"

Fisher turned for a moment to look at his partner. "What's up?"

"Just a minute." She pulled out her phone again and punched in a number. A couple seconds later she said, "Yeah, this dirtbag is with us. Better get in there." She listened for a moment and then said, "You did? Same as Bend? Thanks."

The car pulled out into the fast lane and passed a slower truck. Then Fisher pulled into the right lane and settled back, the white Trooper three cars ahead.

"Talk to me, Harris," Fisher said.

"Two counts of murder," she said to him.

Cliff was terminally confused now. "There was just Jimmy," he said.

She wanted to smack him again. "Jimmy took one to the chest and one to the forehead. Your friend Zack Evans in Bend took one to the back of the head at close range."

Cliff turned white and sunk deep into his seat. His two best friend's were dead because he had wanted to spend a couple extra days with Li. He couldn't believe it. When the tears came, he could do nothing to stop them.

CHAPTER 27

Shemya, Alaska

Two airmen had died on the tarmac when the plane arrived. Senior Airman Cato, a nineteen year old from Del Rio, Texas had been the first to die, taking a single round to the forehead. The other to die was Sergeant Temple, a security policeman from Fresno.

The lone gunman had still not been identified.

The entire detachment of special agents from the Air Force Office of Special Investigations from Elmendorf Air Base in Anchorage had caught a flight and were conducting the investigation. But, Colonel Powers knew there would be more to come, he was sure.

The colonel was in his office behind his desk, making the OSI agent wait in the outer office. He didn't like the cocky special agents, who didn't wear the Air Force uniform, and could have been a sergeant or a captain. Thank God for his new computer system, he thought. While the man waited outside, he had pulled up the agent's record. He was a Captain Dave Eyler, the detachment commander in Elmendorf. What he didn't know, though, was the man who accompanied him. He had simply flashed a badge to his secretary.

He called his secretary and told her to send the two in, but remained behind his desk. He had no intention of letting the power of his position and rank be diminished by the two of them.

Dressed in suits, with pants tucked into Sorels, the two agents came in and stood in front of the colonel's desk. Captain Eyler was short and stocky with a beard that was long even for an OSI special agent. The man to his left was a tall, thin man with a chiseled jaw that jutted out like that cartoon Canadian Mountie.

The colonel considered them in silence. Then he waved his hand toward two cushioned chairs. "Take a seat." It wasn't a request.

They sat and the captain pulled out a small notebook, flipping a few pages.

"Anything on the shooter?" Colonel Powers asked.

The two men looked at each other. The captain was about to speak, but was halted by the colonel standing and approaching them.

"First of all," the colonel said. "I like to know who I'm talking with. Let's see some I.D." He stood there with his hands out.

Without thinking about it, the two men produced their badges.

"And your I.D.s," Colonel Powers said.

They pulled them out and the colonel looked them over carefully before returning them to the men. That's interesting, he thought, as he took a seat behind his desk.

"I understand OSI being here," Powers said, "but why is the Network involved?"

"Is this room secure?" the Network man asked.

"My comm people swept it just before you arrived," Powers assured him. "They're in the process of sweeping every building now."

The Network man seemed pleased with that. "We're involved because of a breech at one of the contractors on this project."

"Which one?" the colonel asked.

"We can't say," Captain Eyler said.

"You can and you will," the colonel told him. "This is my fuckin' project. Anyone has the need to know, it's me."

The two special agents looked at each other. Finally, the captain said, "Brightstar."

"Shit! That's the lead contractor. The software that was just delivered came from them. Same with most of the hardware."

"We know that, Sir," the Network man said. "Our people are working on it now."

Sir? Not bad from a Network weenie. "How?"

"That you don't need to know."

"Fair enough." Colonel Powers had only been trying to push to see how far he could go with them. "What do you guess the shooter was trying to accomplish?"

They both hunched their shoulders, glancing sideways at each other.

"Speculate," the colonel said, more seriously now.

The Network man spoke first. "Could have been working with those in California. We'll know more once we find out who he is."

"Is this espionage homegrown or foreign?" Powers asked.

The OSI captain started to talk, but was shut up with a foot sliding from the Network man.

"We didn't say anything about espionage," the Network man said.

"You just did, boys." The colonel smiled. "You two gotta work out more subtle signals." He hesitated and then said, "Let's cut the bullshit. Just tell me how much of my program has been compromised. And I don't want a long cock and bull tale from you about need to know and we're not sure and all that crap. The test is tomorrow. I need to know that when we go to shoot down phase we got a good chance of hitting our target."

There was a long silence. Then the Network man spoke. "We honestly don't know, Sir."

There came that Sir again. Maybe this wasn't one of those arrogant fucks from Washington. "Now that's an honest answer. I don't like people bullshittin' me. Give me the straight skinny and let me work with it. Good, bad or ugly. So, you don't know who took the Brightstar shit?"

"We know who took it," Network said. "We're not sure why. The guy is being tracked now."

"Trying to lead you to someone?" Powers asked.

"Yes, Sir."

"Which country is involved?" the colonel asked.

The OSI officer looked at the Network man, who said, "Don't know."

"Now, that's a lie Mr. Network man. That's too bad. You were doing great up to that point."

"I can't tell you that," he said.

"The Chinese!"

The Network man's eyes shot up.

"I was just guessing," Colonel Powers said. "But now I guess I got my answer."

"We don't know anything for sure," the Network man said, trying his best to back track.

"That's the truth, Sir," special agent Eyler said.

That was one truth, the colonel knew. But these two would never give him the full story.

CHAPTER 28

The sun was just coming up over the Lesser Khingan Range in northern Manchuria, when Jake and Su reached the valley. They were both exhausted from running most of the night. And, although their clothes had turned from wet to frozen, neither seemed overtly hypothermic.

When they reached a small wooden bridge that crossed the river, they stopped for a moment to catch their breath.

"Which way from here?" Jake asked her.

"We cross the bridge and then it's two miles, maybe more, before we reach my uncle's village."

Jake set his backpack down and searched inside for the camera and phone. He had to get those pictures sent. He turned on the phone and still got no signal.

"What the hell is going on here?" he yelled.

"It should work," she assured him. She pointed off to the southwest. "We put a cell tower some five miles up there." She pulled out her phone and also got no signal.

"Someone must have fucked with your tower," he said.

She nodded her agreement.

"Let's go!"

They packed up and shuffled off across the bridge. They got about halfway across when they saw the helo. Perhaps the same one that had flown over them as they flew down the mountainside into the river a few hours ago.

They were trapped. To turn back, they might make it across the bridge before the helicopter reached them. But then what? To run straight ahead, they would be running toward the helo.

In a split second, they had no choice. Coming from behind them was a military truck. About a mile off in the distance moving fast toward them.

"This way," Jake yelled, pulling her across the bridge.

Just after they reached the other side of the bridge, the helo lowered and turned sideways, its wash blowing snow up everywhere and pushing Jake and Su together.

Jake turned his head, his arm over his eyes, and tried to see how far away the truck was now. It was less than half a mile away.

Turning back toward the helo, he noticed the side door had opened and someone was waving arms, wanting them to approach.

"You know them?" Jake yelled to Su, barely above the rotors and wind.

She looked confused, shaking her head no.

And then he thought he heard something familiar. At first it was almost an echo, and then it became more clear. Jake. The man was yelling his name.

He had only a few seconds to make a choice, because the truck was now on the bridge some fifty yards away. Stopped. Men hopping off with rifles.

Jake pulled on Su's arm and hauled her toward the helo. Things became clearer as Jake got closer. Under the hat and headphones was Brian Armstrong, the Network officer from Beijing.

"Get in," Armstrong yelled at Jake.

"How'd you find us?" Jake asked as he slung his backpack in before helping Su with hers.

"Just get in. They don't look too friendly."

As the Network officer said that, the first bullets started hitting the side of the helo.

Su climbed aboard, struggled to lift her frozen legs, and Jake grabbed her by the pants and shoved her inside. Then he launched himself inside.

Armstrong slammed the door shut and yelled for the pilot to take off. Bullets smacked into the door, and they all dove to the deck.

The helo lifted off and shook about as it turned and swept off to the south.

Jake pulled himself to a sitting position and leaned against his backpack.

"That was close," he yelled to Armstrong.

Something wasn't right. The Network officer lay on his stomach. Still.

Then Jake saw the blood seeping from his lower back. He turned Armstrong over.

"Armstrong. You all right?" Jake shouted.

His eyes were open, but his face said it all. He wasn't all right. His breathing was labored and a stream of blood trickled from the side of his mouth.

Jake turned to Su. "Find a first aid kit. He's been hit."

She searched the compartment while Jake held his hand on the blood spot.

"Can you talk?" Jake asked him.

"I'll be all right," Armstrong said, his words barely making it from his lips. "You get the photos?"

"Yes."

"Don't send them on the phone."

"Why?"

"Compromised."

"I don't get it."

Su came to them with a first aid kit, and pulled out a bandage and tape. As she pulled up his coat to access the wound, Jake lay onto the floor next to Armstrong.

"What do I do with the photos?" Jake asked him.

"Shemya . . . Alaska."

"What about it?"

"Bring it there."

"A Network officer there?"

"No!" He writhed in pain.

Jake looked at Su, who was trying to cover the wound, but was losing the battle. Her hands were full of blood; the compress bandage had turned from white to completely red. And Jake realized she must be in pain herself, with her left wrist broken.

"Who then?" Jake asked.

"Colonel Powers. Only him." Armstrong's eyes started to close.

Jake shook him. "No. Stay awake. How'd you find us?"

"G. . . P. . .S. . . Inside backpack handle."

"Shit! Just hang in there, man." The horror of this was just starting to hit Jake. He had worked with Armstrong's brother in the Ukraine, and that officer had died. Sure Jake had had no part in that, but maybe he could have seen it coming. And now another Armstrong, who was only trying to save his ass, was now dying.

Su pulled on Jake's arm. "I can't stop it."

Armstrong's eyes were now closed; his breathing had stopped. Jake checked for a carotid pulse.

Nothing.

Jake shook his head. "Damn it!" He slammed his hand against the deck.

Su put her hand on Jake's back. "You good friends?"

He shook his head. "No, we just met a few days ago." He hesitated and then said, "It's a long story."

Jake took in deep breaths, trying his best to maintain control. He had to think about their current situation. Who was flying this beast? And where were they heading?

He pulled the headset from Armstrong's head and put it on. Then, through the microphone, he asked, "Hey, you speak English up there?" He could only see the back of the pilot's head, which was covered by a helmet.

The pilot turned around. It was a black man in his 50s. "What the fuck you think, Bitch? What the fuck goin' on back there?"

"Armstrong took a bullet in the back," Jake said.

"He all right?" the pilot asked.

"He's dead."

"Dat ain't all right." The pilot turned back to flying.

Jake moved forward. He saw they were flying low, the trees to the side even with them. Then he saw why. They were following the river downstream.

"I'm Jake Adams."

"I'd shake your hand and all that shit but I'm a little busy right now," the pilot said. "Armstrong told me about you on the flight up. We coulda picked ya up last night in the mountains but we had no way of contacting you. Had to go back for fuel."

"Phones weren't working," Jake said.

The pilot nodded agreement.

"You work for the Network?" Jake asked.

"I work for whoever pays my ass. Been in these parts for more than thirty years. After Nam I just couldn't go back. Damn pussy is just too damn good." He peered around behind him toward Su. "She can't hear this. You get any of that yet? She fine!"

Jake changed the subject. "Where we heading?"

"Changchun for fuel. Then Shenyang. You can catch a flight from there to Beijing."

"What about Armstrong?"

"We had a contingency for all this shit. You let me take care of him. I fly. You get the hell outta China. You better bring her with you?"

"Why?"

The pilot hesitated and then finally said, "They been roundin' up her relatives. She can't go back."

Jake looked to the rear at Su, who was now curled up in a blanket trying to get warm.

What in the hell was going on? This should have been a simple job. Get in, take a few photos, get out. But nothing was ever as easy as that, Jake knew. Now he had to tell Su that she would have to leave China with him. Would she go?

He watched the landscape fly by below as the sun rose higher on the horizon. He had left his stuff in Beijing at the hotel, but he had no real desire to go back for it. It was only clothes. He could get those anywhere.

Glancing back at Armstrong on the deck of the chopper, he wondered how he would ever be able to justify his death to himself or anyone else. And why Alaska of all places? Did it matter? He had already been paid quite nicely, and the job was not over.

He never left anything undone.

CHAPTER 29

Where the hell is she going?" Special Agent Fisher asked aloud to himself as he turned the car onto I-205 North just south of Portland.

It was getting dark, at that period where the eyes had not changed from day to night, and the rain had picked up some. To make matters worse, it was Friday evening and rush hour traffic would become a bigger problem as they approached Portland.

Cliff had his eyes closed in the back seat, and Agent Harris had climbed over to the front passenger seat about ten miles back to help navigate.

"I'm guessing the airport," Harris said. "The two oh five bypasses most of the city and ends up right at Portland International."

"Great. If we don't stick close, she'll end up on a plane to damn near anywhere without us catching her. I say we just pull her ass over. We got her on murder and espionage. What more do we need?"

"You know better than that," Harris said to him. "We need to know who she's working for; otherwise we'll never get it out of her."

Agent Fisher pulled around a couple of cars to get closer to the white Trooper ahead.

"What are you doing? Not so close."

"We lose her and we're fucked."

Harris thought for a minute and then pulled out a map of Portland. She could barely read it, only seeing what she needed from the headlights of cars behind them.

"Okay," Harris said. "We call ahead. Have a reception waiting for her at the airport."

"What if she doesn't go to the airport?" This surprised the both of them, coming from Cliff in the back.

"Shut the fuck up!" Harris said.

"He's got a point," Fisher said under his breath.

She checked the map again. "All right, smart ass. Where do you think she's going?" She turned directly at Cliff; a look that burned right through him.

"Seattle."

"Seattle?" she asked. "Why the fuck Seattle?"

Cliff shrugged. "That's where I'd go. Li is Chinese, right? If she's working for them, then she'd need a flight there to deliver the DVD she got from me."

"And she can't do that from Portland?" Fisher asked.

"There are no direct flights from Portland to China," Cliff assured them. "You have to fly to Seattle, San Fran, or L.A. So, she'd want to pick up a direct flight."

"Why do you assume that?" Harris asked.

Cliff shook his head. "She could have caught a flight to Portland in Eugene, and then another to Seattle. That's if she had wanted a bunch of connections."

Fisher laughed as he pulled out and passed another car.

"All right," Harris said. "But why does she have to deliver the DVD? Why not just send the data over the Internet to China?"

Cliff leaned forward in his seat against the seat belt. "Now here's where I'm sure about her. She doesn't trust technology. She thinks the government is tracking every transfer of data."

Harris glanced sideways at Fisher and then back at Cliff. "Which government?"

"Doesn't matter. All governments."

"Shit!"

"What?" Fisher said.

"Cliff, are you sure you don't know who she works for?" Harris asked him.

"Absolutely. She did make a number of phone calls, though. You might want to have those traced."

"How we gonna do that, dumbass?" Harris asked him. "She's using a cell phone. Probably a throw away."

"Trace her number."

There was silence in the car as Fisher looked at Harris, and then Harris turned to Cliff.

"You have her number?" Harris asked. "Why the hell didn't you tell us that before?"

"You never asked."

Cliff gave her the number and then Harris made a call to the Portland office to have them trace the calls and also tell them their current location.

"How long have you had the number?" Fisher asked him.

"Couple weeks. I stayed at her place one night, picked up her phone, thinkin' it was mine, since it's the same model, and turned it on to make a call. You know how the home number pops up on some models as soon as you turn them on? Well, I remembered the number." He pulled out his cell phone from his pocket. "You wanna give her a call? We could ask her where she's going. Save us some time."

Suddenly, Fisher braked hard to avoid a car that had done the same in front of them. He swerved to the fast lane to keep from hitting an old pickup truck. Then he hit the gas to get around the vehicle to keep up with the Trooper.

"Damn it!" Fisher said. "I think she caught us. She tapped on her brakes."

"Let's give her a call," Cliff said, proud of his thought.

"I told you to shut the fuck up," Harris yelled back at him. "I'm gonna have to climb back there and baby-sit your ass."

"That's all right," Cliff said, rubbing his jaw, which had swollen considerably. "Got da picture."

Then, without warning, the white Trooper turned off onto an exit that led to an overpass and started to slow.

"Hang on folks," Fisher said. "Something's up."

The Trooper pulled over to the side of the ramp at the top of the hill. Fisher had two choices. He could simply pull up behind her, or he could pass by and turn right. Seconds to decide.

Pull behind her.

He came to a stop a couple of car lengths behind the Trooper and kept the engine running, the wipers swishing to remove the rain.

By the time anyone knew what was happening, it was too late. The driver's door on the Trooper opened. A figure appeared for a moment. There were five flashes of light. And then the door closed and the Trooper sped off.

There were shards of glass everywhere in the front seat. Fisher was the first to raise his head above the dash.

The Trooper was gone.

"What the fuck happened?" Cliff yelled from the back seat.

Fisher put the car in gear and sped off after the Trooper. He thought he saw the tail lights go straight across the highway and back onto the freeway, but he wasn't entirely sure.

When he finally had a chance to look to his right, he saw that Agent Harris was slumped over.

"Oh, God."

He pulled over to the side of the road on the on-ramp.

"Harris!" he yelled at her, checking her for wounds. She had taken a round in her left shoulder. The shock had knocked her out, he was sure. He held his hand over the wound. "Use that damn phone of yours to call an ambulance," he screamed at Cliff.

CHAPTER 30

Shenyang, China

As the chopper flew off to the southwest toward Beijing, Jake and Su shuffled with their backpacks from the field toward the narrow road that led to a small village. Jake knew they could hop a train from there. The Network pilot had thought it best to not fly them directly to the Shenyang airport. None of them wanted the police to discover an American contract pilot flying two people on the run, not to mention the dead body of an American embassy diplomat. Besides, the air traffic controllers had undoubtedly been told of the helo that had been shot up, and would be watching for them.

It was almost noon. Jake walked alongside the deserted road behind Su, whose left arm hung at her side as if it were dead. He knew the broken wrist would have to be set soon or it wouldn't heal properly. If she waited much longer, the doctor would have to re-break it and then set it.

She was having a hard time with the heavy backpack, so Jake stepped up and stopped her.

"Let me help you with your pack," he said to her.

"I can handle it," she answered emphatically. Tears streaked her face.

"You're not all right," Jake said.

"Has nothing to do with my wrist."

That's what Jake thought. He had been forced to relay the information about her family being rounded up.

"You can't turn yourself in," Jake told her. "You'll never see the light of day."

"They never see light either."

Jake knew that might be true, but maybe not. "Listen, if you drop off the face of the Earth, what can they do? They can't hold your family forever."

"Chinese are patient people. Communists more patient." She started walking again, determined.

He'd work on her. But right now they had to keep moving. In a mile or so they came across the small village that was linked better by rail than road. In fact, much of Manchuria was linked better by rail.

It wasn't hard to find the rail station. But after Su bought two tickets to Shenyang and came back to where Jake was sitting on a small wooden bench in the tiny terminal, she informed him they'd have an hour to wait for the next train.

She took a seat next to him, her backpack at her feet. "Sorry about my emotions," she said.

"Hey, nothing to be sorry about. We don't know for sure that the government has your family. Would they link you to your friend in Harbin?"

She sat stone faced and said, "I know now. Heard my name on the radio when I picked up the tickets."

Jake let out a deep breath. "I'm sorry."

"You did nothing."

"I got you into this."

"No. I did this. I could have said no."

That might have been true, but Jake was sure the Network probably had some leverage against her. Something that forced her hand.

"Will it be safe to go to Shenyang?" Jake asked her.

"I don't know. But we can't get to Alaska without catching a flight from Shenyang to an international airport."

"Are you going with me?"

She nodded her head. "I don't have a choice."

Jake glanced across the room at the man behind the ticket counter, who had just picked up the phone and set it back down again, and was showing too much interest in their conversation. Other than the two of them, the place was empty. Something wasn't right.

On their way in, Jake had noticed a small car parked out back; a Volkswagen Santana, Shanghai's version of a 1980s Jetta.

Su glanced up at Jake as he rose and walked toward the ticket counter, not understanding what was happening.

With one fluid motion, Jake grabbed the man by the shirt and slammed him to the counter. Then he swung his legs over the counter and punched the man once in the kidney, dropping him to his knees. Once he had the guy on his face on the floor, trying to catch his breath, Jake riffled through the man's pockets.

"What the hell you doing?" Su yelled. She had run across the room to the other side of the counter.

"He was going to call the cops on us. Come here!"

She came around the side of the counter.

"Grab that tape over there. And the scissors."

She did as he said, handing them to him. In less than a minute, Jake had the man tied up and taped from head to toe. He wouldn't be going anywhere for a while. At least not until the next train came and they found him there. He checked his watch. That gave them forty-five minutes.

"Let's go," he said.

They collected their backpacks and hurried outside.

"What about the train?" Su asked.

Jake pulled out a set of keys and led her to the crappy, beat up car in the back lot.

"You're getting good at stealing cars," she said. "You sure you don't do this for a living?"

He opened the driver's door. "Nope. But everybody has to have a hobby."

Getting in, he unlocked the other doors and they put the packs in the back seat.

"Where we going now?" she asked, sitting in the passenger seat.

He cranked over the car and shrugged. "You're asking me? This is your country."

"Shenyang is that way," she said, pointing toward the south.

"Great."

He pulled back, ground the gears, put it in first gear, and shot away from the terminal.

After they got out onto a main road heading toward Shenyang, Jake considered what to do. They had to leave China as soon as possible. But their choices were limited. There would be no direct flights to Alaska. They'd have to fly to Seattle or San Francisco. But maybe. He smiled at his idea. It wasn't the first time he had thought of it, though. When Armstrong and Anderson had first recruited him for this job, he had considered the option that he might be hung out to dry. After all, that's why they had hired him in the first place. They could disavow any knowledge of his existence. He was, as they would say, not affiliated with the U.S. government in any way. So, he had always known he might need another way out of China. Now it was time to call in an old favor.

Traffic on the main road got heavier as they closed in on the city of six million people.

"How far?" Jake asked. "What'd that last sign say?"

"About five miles."

"I hope you're ready for another road trip."

She looked confused. "We can catch a flight to Beijing here. Be there in time for evening meal."

He shook his head. "No, they'll be watching the airport. They'll expect that. We'll do the unexpected. With the right traffic, we'll be there by late evening." That is, if the car held up, he thought.

When they got to an outer ring of Shenyang, Jake drove around the east side of the city, not even catching more than a glimpse of small Hutongs on the outskirts.

CHAPTER 31

There had been no choice. Fisher had thought his new partner had taken a shot to her shoulder, but the bullet had actually struck her just below her left shoulder socket, ripping a hole through her left biceps. Another shot had hit her directly in the chest, sinking deep into her Kevlar vest, and taking her breath away for a moment. With Harris hit, Fisher had driven her to the closest hospital in the Portland area, dropping her at the emergency room door, and then speeding off after the Asian woman in the white Trooper.

Fisher would have been quite angry had they not placed the satellite tracker on the Trooper while it sat in front of the house in Eugene. He had just gotten off the phone with the Portland office; they had relayed the woman's position to him.

The more difficult part had been swapping cars, since theirs had been shot up and the windshield destroyed. They had coordinated an exchange on the side of Interstate 205 just before it crossed over the Columbia River, and were now in a huge Crown Victoria. That didn't satisfy Fisher, since the car was purchased by mostly police departments or old folks.

As he suspected, the Asian woman had passed up the Portland International Airport exit and crossed the Columbia River into Washington.

"You won't catch her," Cliff said from the back seat. "She's smart, man. Really smart."

"Shut the fuck up, Cliff." Fisher was still kicking himself for not dropping him off at the hospital. But, at the time, his partner, Agent Harris, had been in no condition to baby-sit the guy. Besides, he felt responsible for all that had happened. If he had caught on to Cliff Johansen sooner, none of this would have happened. That was one way to look at it. The other, and the one that would stand up in court, was that he couldn't have stopped Cliff for espionage until he had actually taken the Brightstar information. How was he to know that the guy would make a run for it? Most spies hung around for a while to make sure they would not arouse suspicion, or at least to squeeze more money out of their runners. But Cliff's motivation had been both money and sex. As it turned out, sex might have been just as important to him.

"I'm sorry, man," Cliff said.

Fisher checked him out in the rearview mirror. "You're sorry all right. What the hell were you thinking?"

"I meant about your partner gettin' shot. I didn't think it would ever come to this."

"It almost always comes to this," Fisher told him.

A cell phone rang and Fisher picked it up from inside his jacket pocket. "Yeah." He listened carefully and then said thanks before hanging up.

"How is she?"

"It wasn't about Harris," Fisher said. He picked up the map and threw it to the back seat. "Here. Make yourself useful. Your partner is near Chehalis. We just passed mile marker fifty-nine. Do the math."

"Hey, ya got me cuffed to the door back here. How the hell ya expect me ta. . ."

"Cliff!"

"Twenty-two miles."

Fisher calculated that in his mind. She was traveling under the radar at sixty-four miles an hour. He was pushing the limit at eighty-two. That means. Damn, he hated those math problems.

"If she's going the speed limit," Cliff said, "which I'm sure she is, then you'll catch her somewhere between Olympia and Tacoma. Unless you slow down for Olympia."

"Shut up, Cliff."

"Hey, you asked, Pal. I gotta piss, by the way."

"Let's see," Fisher said, "a man gets thrown from a car traveling eighty-two miles an hour. How far do his brains splatter?"

"Funny." Then Cliff mumbled something under his breath.

Traffic started to pick up somewhat, but the fast lane remained fairly calm. Fisher only had to slow a few times until he flashed his brights behind a slow poke who lingered where he shouldn't. The biggest problem was the rain, which went from anywhere from a few sprinkles to a complete downpour without warning. Which it was doing right now, making it almost impossible to maintain speed.

"You're gonna kill us, Steve. Excuse me. Agent Fisher. Or whatever your name is this week."

"Keep talkin' Cliff and I'll make sure you get a huge cell mate. I think you know what I mean."

"Fuckin' A."

"Exactly."

That kept his mouth shut for a while. Fisher tried his best to concentrate, but the smell and the sight of Harris's blood lingered in his mind. He knew she would be all right, though. In fact, at the hospital, she had gotten out of the car herself and walked the last few feet to the emergency room, banging her hand on the roof of the Taurus and telling him to catch the bitch, before slamming the door. He could simply have the Asian woman stopped ahead. Set up a road block between two long stretches of highway where she would have no choice but to stop. That's what the Portland office had wanted to do, but Fisher had convinced them that they needed to know where she was going. Who she was working for. Nothing else mattered now.

"Why's she going to Seattle, Cliff?"

"Don't know. Maybe she likes Sea-Tac."

"Maybe you like another punch in the mouth."

"Damn. When did you become such a bad ass?"

"Maybe because I had to repress my masculinity for so long pretending to be a programmer."

"Thanks."

"No problem."

There was silence for a moment as the windshield wipers swished their music back and forth.

Finally, Cliff broke the quiet. "I didn't mean for this to happen. It just did."

"Do you know what happens if the Chinese get this technology?" Fisher asked.

"I didn't think about that."

"Think about it now. It would negate our laser superiority. If they sold the technology to Russia or any other country, we might as well scrap our systems."

"And that's a bad thing," Cliff said. "Maybe I should have posted it on the Internet. Then every country would have to get rid of their nukes. Maybe I'll still do it."

"What do you mean?" Fisher glanced back through the rearview mirror.

"Nothing."

"You have copies?"

Cliff was silent.

"You have copies," Fisher repeated.

"Hey, Li never said it was an exclusive deal. I thought I'd make a little extra selling to the highest bidder."

"You set up an Internet auction? You're fuckin' incredible. When does this happen?"

"You're a smart guy. Figure it out."

When would be the moment of greatest worth? Fisher struggled with that as he passed a semi trailer that nearly knocked the Crown Victoria off the road. Once he got in front of the truck it came to him. "Right after a successful test," Fisher said. Shit! The test of the new software in Alaska was tomorrow. They needed to stop the test. Or at least delay it.

CHAPTER 32

Jake drove on into the night, while Chang Su slept in the passenger seat. They were just a few miles out of Dandong, a port city of some two million, across the Yalu River from Sinuiju, North Korea. Jake had chosen the city for a couple of reasons. First, nobody would expect them to go there. There was, after all, no large international airport. It was a port city of little concern to most. Also, Jake was hoping they'd be able to catch a regional flight that wouldn't attract much attention. On the down side, he knew, tourists had not started flocking there yet-at least not in numbers like those heading to Beijing, Shanghai, Xi'an, Guilin, and Yangtze River cruises. He would stick out.

Su started to wake as the lights from the city started to pass by their windows.

"Where are we?" she asked.

"Just outside of Dandong. I could use your help."

"Sure." She sat up in her seat. "What you need?"

"We need to find the airport."

"There," she said, pointing to a sign ahead. "What time is it?"

Jake took the turn toward the airport. "Why?"

"If it's after ten, the airport will be closed."

He pulled the car to the side of the road and stopped, the engine sputtering and almost shutting down. He ran his fingers through his hair and realized that it had been a long few days. He needed a place to sleep. A place to take a shower. And he needed a place that would not take his passport, or even care about his personal information. Better yet, he thought, he could use one of his additional passports. Since he moved to Austria a few years back, he had gotten a passport under that country.

Nobody questioned an Austrian passport in Europe. But here, it would be a novelty that would be easily remembered. It would have to do, though. He was too tired to get original.

He put the car in gear and drove a few blocks to the Bravo Airport Hotel, a large European-style place. In an isolated part of the parking lot, the two of them found more appropriate clothes from their backpacks and checked in as a couple.

When they got to their room on the fourth floor, with a view of the airport, Jake realized there was only one bed, and it was not even a queen size.

"I guess I've got the floor," Jake said to her.

Her eyes seemed dazed, as if she hadn't even considered the sleeping arrangements.

"You mind if I shower first?" he asked.

"That's fine."

Jake got into the small bathroom and stripped from his clothes. He had been on the run for so long, he could only imagine how good the shower would feel.

Naked and standing under the hot water, he ran the soap over his body, the steam rising up in the small room. It was the first time since Beijing that he had gotten a spontaneous erection.

Seconds later, the shower curtain moved aside and Su stepped into the tub, completely naked. She didn't say a word, but her brows rose when she saw him like that.

She got wet and he rubbed the soap over her body, bringing her nipples to match his rigidity. When she first touched him, he thought he would explode. But he willed himself to wait. He had observed her for the last few days, imagining what she would look like under all those clothes. And now. His imagination had not done her justice. She was so perfect. Her skin was as smooth as jade, yet as warm as a hearth.

She shifted her head up to him and he wiped her wet hair to the side of her face, clearing drops of water from her dark eyes.

As their lips touched for the first time, he felt a spark within him that he had not felt in quite some time. They lingered like that, the water running down their heads.

He reached around behind her and lifted her to him.

Sliding down onto him, she gasped.

Together, as one, he helped her rise and fall onto him, until, as if they had synchronized the final act, she writhed with pleasure and he burst into her.

♦

Much later, they lay in bed together, her head against his bare chest, the darkness broken only by a strip of light from the airport.

Jake had had time to think, trying his best to understand what had just happened. He knew that sometimes it was better not to find reasons for some things. Just accept them as they were. He hadn't had the normal hints that they were heading in this direction. Perhaps that was because they had both been focused on the job at hand and the long journey and the death of her friend in Harbin. Although he had been intrigued by her from the first moment they met, he also knew that working closely with someone in his world often clouded his judgment to the real task at hand.

"What you think?" she asked him, barely above a whisper.

"I'm glad you decided to join me."

She turned her head to look him in the eye. "I meant about tomorrow," she said. "I don't expect anything else. I needed." She hesitated, her breathing slowed and her eyes shifting away from his. "I need to feel something good so I'm human again."

He held her tighter. "I understand. You lost a good friend in Harbin."

"You lost Armstrong," she said, as if they were equal.

"True. But we barely knew each other. I feel responsible for his death, though. If I had called him, kept him informed, maybe he wouldn't have had to come looking for us."

She put her hand on his mouth. "No. It was his job. You were doing him a favor. And, they would have caught us if he did not come."

He held her hand. "I know. But first his brother dies in the Ukraine and now. . ."

"Not your fault." Her voice was more serious now.

"Did you know Armstrong?"

She shook her head. "I knew about him, but I worked through a man in Shanghai."

Jake already knew this. At least as far as he was told by Armstrong's man, Anderson.

"Now what?" she asked him.

"Are we talkin' about us or tomorrow?"

She laughed for the first time, and it was appealing. "Tomorrow."

"Well, we have to get out of China. I have a friend in Korea. If we can get there, he can help us."

Her smile turned to a gravity he had not seen in her.

"It'll be all right," he assured her.

"Not all right. I have to leave my country for good."

"You left for college."

"Yes, but I came back. They might kill my family."

Jake shook his head. "No. We'll plant a story. They'll think you're dead."

She looked at him as if they had just conspired to an actual murder. "You can do that?"

"I can make sure it happens."

Sighing deeply, she dug her face into his chest and wrapped her arm tightly around his back.

They lay there like that, her falling asleep first, and Jake wondering if he could get them out of the country and then out of Korea. He would have to make it happen. He had to get the shots he took to Alaska. Keep his promise to Armstrong.

CHAPTER 33

Seattle, Washington

Parked on South Washington Street, a half a block back from the white Trooper, Fisher had watched Li jump out and climb a set of steps, going into an old brick building that appeared to be a mix of businesses and apartments. They were in the heart of the Pioneer Square section of downtown Seattle, a few blocks from Pike Street Market. Even at this late hour, nearly midnight, the streets were alive with people and cars.

A homeless man approached and knocked on Fisher's window. He powered the window down.

"Get lost!" Fisher growled at the man.

This didn't phase the guy, so Fisher pulled out his gun and pointed it in the man's face.

The man moved his head closer to the 9mm automatic. "Is that any way to treat your back up?" The man flipped his hand sideways, revealing a Network badge. "Just give me a five and send me on my way. I'll be across the street on that bench. We've got the back covered and two more out front. A couple."

Fisher handed the guy a five and pushed him back from the car, closing the window.

"You guys are fucked up," Cliff said from the back seat. He was laying down with a coat over him.

"Listen. Anything goes down here and you better stay put or I'll hunt your ass down."

"You got me cuffed to the door. Where could I go?"

Good point. Fisher was confused by the woman's actions. Just before coming here, the Asian woman had stopped at a used music shop, pounded on the door for a moment, and then, more than a little pissed off that the place was closed, had hopped back into the Trooper and sped off. "What in the hell is she up to, Cliff?"

"How should I know?"

"Ya fucked her."

"Yeah, but she mostly did the fucking. It's not like she gave me any information. The flow went from me to her and not the other way."

"Hang on."

A man and woman walked past and seemed to stare for too long. Must have been the couple, Fisher thought.

Fisher kept his eyes on the door to the brick building, only shifting away to scan the Trooper against the curb in front of them.

It must have been at one of those brief moments when his eyes had turned away when she came out the front door, because when he first saw her she was skipping down the stone steps and then getting into the Trooper.

Fisher's phone rang. Picking up, he said, "Yeah." He listened for a moment, watching the brake lights on the Trooper shine brightly. "I can't get the cuffs off and still follow her. As you can see, she's leaving right now." He listened and put the car in gear, pulling out after the Trooper. "Gotcha." Then he flipped the phone into his pocket.

"You tryin' to get rid of me?" Cliff said.

"Not now."

Fisher followed the Trooper around a corner, keeping way back. They drove up the hill underneath I-5 and then north, parallel to the freeway.

"Where the hell are you going, Bitch?" Fisher said to himself.

Cliff sat up in the back seat. "I told you. The airport."

"She's goin' in the opposite direction," Fisher said.

The phone rang and Fisher tried to ignore it, but it wouldn't go away. Finally he picked up and listened. "Shit! We should have taken her there." Pause. "Gotcha." He hung up.

"What?" Cliff asked.

"Your friend just killed two people in that apartment. A young Chinese couple."

Cliff sank into his seat.

Fisher kept the car back, not wanting her to see them, yet on one level he hoped she'd pull over like she had in Portland. Give him another chance to take her out. But he knew they needed more from her. Needed to find out who employed her. Without that knowledge, all of his work over the past few months would have been for no reason. All that time schmoozin' with computer geeks a lesson in futility.

The Trooper turned right up a hill and picked up speed. When it reached a heavily treed area by Seattle University, it slowed and pulled over to a curb.

Fisher held back, took a right on the first street on the edge of a campus park and then pulled over and hit the lights. He was careful not to put pressure on the brakes to give away his position.

Almost a block away, through the trees, Fisher watched the woman get out of the Trooper and hurry into the campus park, her gate purposeful. Was she going to kill someone else? This had to stop.

He pulled his phone out and called his Portland boss, relayed his position, and told him he needed back-up at this location.

"What do you mean not yet," Fisher said loudly. "She just killed two people in Seattle. Who knows what the hell she's up to now." He listened for a moment, his head nodding agreement. "That's good news." A pause. "She what? She's crazy. Right. Gotcha. Give me her number." He listened carefully now, his eyes closed for a moment to memorize the sequence of numbers. "Got it. Thanks."

Fisher hung up and returned his phone to his pocket.

"Was that about your friend?" Cliff asked. "She okay?"

Fisher tried to ignore the little puke in the back seat, but he just wouldn't go away. Like a cockroach, he was. "Better than expected. Treated and released. Bullet missed the major artery in her arm. The Kevlar stopped the one in her chest, but she'll have one helluva bruise."

"I guess large breasts come in handy," Cliff noted.

Fisher ignored that and checked his watch. His back-up, those who would take this annoying geek off his hands, were about five minutes out. He only hoped the Asian woman, Li, would wait at least that long before jumping back into the Trooper and heading off to who knows where.

Where was she?

The first indication Fisher had that something was not right happened so fast he couldn't comprehend what was going on.

The first bullet smashed through the rear window.

Fisher ducked and pulled his gun in one motion. If the shooter was right outside the car, she could just walk up and it would be like shooting fish in a barrel. He had to move.

Leaning down, he cranked over the engine and shoved it in gear. Then he hit the gas, lurching the car forward. He sat up just before crashing into the back of a truck and cranked the wheel hard to the left, running up the curb and into the park's grassy bank.

He jumped out and crouched behind the door.

Nothing.

A Chevy Impala rounded the corner and headed toward them. He jumped out into the street, aiming his gun at the driver until he jammed his brakes and stopped.

Running to the driver, Fisher realized it was his back-up, the agent dressed in homeless garb.

"What's going on?" the Network officer asked.

"The bitch just shot at us," Fisher yelled. "Was the Trooper gone from that street?" He pointed off across the park.

"Didn't see it."

"Shit." Fisher finally looked around at his car and saw Cliff slumped over in the back seat.

Hurrying to him, Fisher opened the back door. There was blood everywhere. The bullet had taken off a chunk of Cliff's head. But he checked for a pulse. He was still alive.

By now, the homeless agent was behind him.

"Give me your keys," Fisher ordered.

"But. . ."

"Give me your fuckin' keys and call an ambulance."

The man did as Fisher asked. Then he jumped into the Chevy Impala and powered the window down.

"Stick with him. I'm going after her."

With that, Fisher slammed it into gear and turned the large vehicle around. When he finally hit the gas hard, he realized the extra power he had at his disposal. The car burst with energy as he came to the street where Li had left the Trooper.

It was gone. That was actually a good thing. If she had changed vehicles, he would have had no way of tracking her.

He called in for her position.

CHAPTER 34

Shemya, Alaska

Colonel Powers paced across the living room in the small bachelor officer's quarters apartment across from the officers' club. It was close to midnight, and he knew he shouldn't be there. Yet, after his marriage had failed years ago, with no children to show for his thirteen year union, he had become more and more focused on his career in the Air Force. He knew he was taking a chance now just being in the same apartment with another officer under his command. Impropriety was as much a matter of perception as it was with the actual reality of the situation. That's what he had always told his junior officers when they had strayed. Something told him, something deep within himself, that he needed to take this chance. Life was too short and he was too close to retirement to care that much anyway. With twenty-two years under his belt, he could walk away at any time. That's how he felt on one level. But he still couldn't help wonder if there was a star in his future, assuming his current mission was favorable. He had a chance to make history in Alaska.

He glanced around the curtains at the airfield, frozen solid, the lights from the runway shining off the crystallized snow.

When he heard a noise behind him, he turned to see her cross the room with a drink in each hand. Her dark hair flowed back in rivulets with each step, her wide smile somewhat hesitant.

"Two vodka martinis, Sir." She handed one to him and raised hers for a toast. "To warmth in this frozen tundra."

They touched glasses and each took a short sip. Then she sat down onto the sofa, her dark eyes still penetrating what must have been total uncertainty in him. My God, he thought, this is Sara Chavez, a captain that he had first worked with in Colorado Springs when he was a rising major waiting to pin on lieutenant colonel, and she was a second lieutenant right out of ROTC.

She patted the sofa. “Sir, please take a seat.”

He hesitated. “Sara, try not to call me Sir. We’re off duty.”

“That’s gonna be hard. But I’ll try.” She thought for a moment. “We’re just having a drink here. It’s not like we’re havin’ sex.”

His heart raced with that thought, and he had to admit to himself that he had considered that option even back in Colorado while he was still married. Maybe he needed to feel alive again. Feel wanted by a woman. Especially a woman as beautiful as Sara Chavez. Reluctantly, he came around the coffee table and sat on the couch a few feet away from his captain.

“We’ve had drinks before,” Sara said to him.

“Official parties,” Powers said. “Once in a while with other officers out on the town. This seems different.”

“Does that bother you? We’ve known each other for seven years. I’m thirty years old. Quite single. You’re divorced. Quite divorced. Two adults who have a lot in common.”

“But you work for me.”

She took a sip of her martini and set the glass on the coffee table, shaking her head. “Let’s say we work together. Let’s say we both work for the government. It’s not like I’m gonna slack off just because we’ve had a few drinks. You know me.”

That was true. She had to be the hardest working officer he had known. A true professional. Which is one reason he had been surprised when she asked him to come here after drinks with the entire officer corps earlier in the evening. He had said yes without thinking about the consequences. Could he forget about them now?

Her eyes seemed to glisten and penetrate him. She was a mesmerizing beauty, that was no doubt.

He needed to change the subject. “It’s hard to believe what happened this morning,” he said.

She let out a deep breath. “Is there any motive?”

“OSI is investigating, along with the Network.”

“Really. The Network’s involved?”

He sipped his martini. She did a great job on that, he thought. “I don’t have to tell you the importance of this test. You'll make major first time up just being involved with this project."

"You could get your first star."

Not if anyone found out he was fraternizing with one of his captains, he thought. "I'm not too worried about that," he said. He didn't want to mention that he had been offered a job by two separate defense contractors for much more than he made now. That, with a colonel's retirement, would set him up nicely for the rest of his life. But what good was money if he couldn't share his success with someone else?

"Will we have to delay the test?" she asked.

"Just a few days while the OSI investigates," he said, and then finished off his drink and set the empty glass on the table. "You know them. They see conspiracies behind everything."

She quickly finished her martini to catch up with him. "Let's have another."

Before he could respond, she got up and walked back to the kitchen. Damn. What a fine ass. In fact, he couldn't find one flaw in her.

From the other room she said, "Shaken, not stirred, right?" She poked her head around the corner and smiled.

He caught himself smiling back.

"I knew you had that in you," she said, returning to the task at hand.

Moments later she returned carrying two more drinks. This time she sat down closer to him, placing the martini in his hand, and her hand staying longer on his to make sure he had the glass.

"Sara, can I ask you a personal question?" Colonel Powers asked.

"Of course."

He hesitated, choosing his words carefully. "You are a beautiful woman. Why. . ."

"Don't I have a husband?"

He laughed. "I was thinking boyfriend, but yeah."

She ran her fingers through her long hair, pushing it away from her eyes. "As you know, I had a boyfriend in Colorado for a while. It didn't work out. He was a civilian. Didn't understand my passion for the military. And I did work some crazy hours."

"And now?"

She shrugged. "Now we've been here a few months, and there aren't many men I might be interested in here."

"None worthy?"

She laughed. "You could say that."

There was a long silence, with both uncertain how to proceed.

"Now, can I ask you a personal question?" she said.

"Sure."

"Are you going to kiss me?"

He didn't need any more prompting. He took her glass from her hand and set both of them on the table, and with the next move he closed in and kissed her passionately. Together they rolled back to a laying position on the sofa, still embraced.

He ran his hands through her hair and she grabbed his strong biceps.

They didn't say another word as they rose and left a trail of clothes all the way to her bedroom. Seven years of sexual tension exploded from each of them. Twice in the first half hour.

♦

Colonel Powers lay on his side in her bed, her clock radio reading ten after one in the morning. He knew he should get back to his quarters, but he didn't want to go. She had gotten up to go to the bathroom adjoining the bedroom.

When she stepped out and the light shone on her beautiful smooth skin and hard body, she stood for a moment gazing at him in her bed. Her nipples were hard from the chill in the air.

"I think you're standing at attention," he said to her with a laugh.

She looked down and then rubbed each nipple seductively between her fingers. "The question is," she said with a soft voice, "are you at attention yet?"

He looked under the sheets, and happy with what he found, revealed himself to her.

"Now that's something I wanna get straight between us," she said, moving to the bed. "Again."

She crawled in next to him and immediately took him in her hand. "I hope you don't mind deferring command for a while."

He wasn't sure what she meant until she got on top and set herself down onto him. "No problem," barely came from his lips as she rose up and down on him.

CHAPTER 35

Washington, D.C.

A light snow fell onto the quiet Georgetown street, the iron lamps that lined the cobblestone sidewalk still lit in the early dawn. At five a.m. there was little activity in the expensive row houses; the only sign of life came from the homes of high-ranking government officials like White House Chief of Staff Karl Oestreich, who had been making a million dollars a year before trading his job as a communications lobbyist for his considerably smaller federal paycheck.

Sitting out front of Oestreich's three-story brick brownstone house was a black Mercedes sedan with white government plates, the driver peering up from time to time to see if Oestreich was coming. A half a block down the road was a Chevy Suburban with two security agents, drinking coffee, and trying their best to stay awake.

Across the street, hesitant, General Boles unbuckled his seat belt and got out of his dark blue BMW, waited with his door open as he glanced at Oestreich's driver, and then silently closed the door and crossed the street. His Oxfords made the trek difficult, his feet slipping and almost toppling him a couple of times. Once he got to the cobblestones, the footing was much better.

Boles pulled his trench coat tighter against the falling snow, and then waved at the Chief of Staff's driver with his leather-gloved hand before heading up the steps to the front door. The driver, a former FBI special agent, lifted his strong chin with recognition, and then pointed to his watch, as if to say they would be late. Tell the old man to get his butt in gear.

Boles smiled at the man and then continued to the thick wooden outer door. He rang the bell and waited, glancing back once toward the security SUV.

It was the first time General Boles had been there, but he immediately noticed that Oestreich must have made a few modifications to the original building. All of the glass was security grade. The inner door, which would have been wood and glass, was solid wood and probably reinforced internally with bulletproof steel. The locks were top-notch. And the security camera, barely visible, which he looked into now, sat securely in a corner behind tinted glass. Boles smiled.

Just as Boles was about to ring again, he saw the inner door open, with Karl Oestreich standing there in his dress pants and white T-shirt. Seconds later, Oestreich, a confused expression, opened the outer door for him.

"Wayne. What's up?"

"I think your driver's getting impatient."

"Screw him. Come on in."

The general lowered his head and then followed his old friend into his house, the doors closing securely behind them.

The place was wood, stone and tile. Everything of the finest quality.

"What's going on?" Oestreich asked him. "Pardon me. You want a cup of coffee?"

"No, thanks. I won't keep you long."

The two of them stood staring at each other.

Finally, General Boles said, "We lost Armstrong in China."

"What?" The chief of staff's expression changed from settled to concerned. "How?"

"He was shot retrieving Jake Adams."

"Is Adams all right?"

"Yes."

"And his information?"

"He wasn't able to transfer it to Armstrong," Boles said. "We were using a contract pilot. We couldn't expect Adams to turn it over to him."

The chief of staff rubbed his left temple. "Where's Adams now?"

"That's the problem," Boles said. "He was supposed to fly to Beijing and transfer what he had to our folks there."

"And?"

"And he never showed. He and the Chinese agent are gone."

"Gone?"

"Missing."

Oestreich said, "Great!"

"He was supposed to transfer the images by cell phone, but that didn't work. We don't know why."

"You were depending on Chinese cell service?"

"We couldn't give him a satellite phone. If caught, he'd be pegged as a spy in a heartbeat. The phone we gave him was secure, and the number would relay through one of our satellites to our embassy in Beijing."

"Do you know what he has?"

The general shook his head. "No. There's no way of knowing how far along they might be."

"They stole the hardware for our laser system under the last administration," Oestreich said, "and I won't let them get the software under my watch."

"What about the breach at Brightstar?" the general asked, and immediately regretted having done so. Yet, judging from the surprised expression on the chief of staff's face, his intel had been correct.

"Don't know what you're talking about."

"Karl. How long have we known each other?"

Disgusted, Oestreich said, "Jesus H. Christ. Where the hell do you get your information?"

Boles shrugged. "We all have our little network."

"Yeah, well, I think we need you in the big Network."

Laughing, Boles said, "And take a huge pay cut like you? I don't think so. So, the breach. . ."

"Our Network is working it. It looks like the Chinese, though."

"I heard a transfer has been made and they're on the run. Will that impact our test in Alaska?"

The chief of staff pointed his finger at the general's chest. "See. You're already talking like you work for us."

Boles waited somewhat impatiently for an answer, his eyes intense and watching the other man's eyes for the truth.

Oestreich reluctantly said, "The test is delayed."

"Why? We want the Chinese to know our laser system works. Why else did we shoot down the Russian missile?"

"It's complicated. We want them to know about the airborne laser, with its more limited capability."

"But not the Alaskan system that'll knock down anything they could ever develop."

Oestreich was silent, his eyes shifting toward the floor.

"Well?" Boles said. "We could stop all missile development in the world if all of our laser systems work."

Maybe that was the problem, Boles thought. America sold a lot of weapons to our friends around the world. If they thought those weapons were useless, they would stop buying.

Finally, Oestreich said, "The laser works as advertised. It's the software we need to worry about. If the Chinese get that. . ."

"They'll have what we have," Boles said. "Taiwan falls in a week, scooped back up into a true One China."

"That's one concern. Think beyond that, though. China becomes a Superpower without having to spend a shitload of money developing nukes. They don't have to worry about missiles from Russia, missiles from India, or missiles from rogue states. With the largest market in the world, the entire world economy shifts from America to China. We'll become a footnote in history."

Boles thought hard about that, not even seriously considering that possibility.

"We can't let that happen," the chief of staff said emphatically.

CHAPTER 36

Dandong, China

Jake's first understanding that all was not all right came with a quiet click at the door latch. Had he not gotten up from bed to go to the bathroom for a glass of water, he would have been sound asleep.

With the click, though, Jake glanced over to find Su in bed, one leg hanging from the sheet. He left the bathroom light on, but left the door open only a crack to shine some light into the room as he moved over toward the door clothed only in his underwear.

The first thing he saw was a gun, silenced, inching into their room. With one quick movement, he shoved his shoulder into the door, knocking the gun to the floor.

The intruder let out a yell as his hand crunched between door and door frame. Jake jammed it again, but the hand had retreated. He fumbled with the lock. It wouldn't go.

Then the door shoved in on him with great force, knocking him back into the room.

By now, Su had woken and let out a gasp as she pulled the sheet up to cover her nakedness.

Jake recovered, catching the first man in the sternum with a kick. The thrust knocked the first man into the second one, pushing them back a couple of feet.

Moving to his left, Jake caught the second man with a kick to the knee. There was a snap as he dislocated cartilage, bringing the man to his one good knee.

The first man hit Jake in the head with a backfist, dazing him slightly.

Su gave up her dignity and leapt from bed, her first strike a kick to the gunman's groin. Then she swiveled and rear-kicked the other man in his forehead, hurtling him backwards out the door.

Jake sent an elbow into the head of the man eating his own balls. The man, the first gunman, struggled to depart, helping his friend to his feet. Together they mumbled and went off into the early morning darkness.

Slamming the door shut, Jake jammed a chair under the door latch and turned to find Su still in a fighting stance, her breathing heavy. He wanted to linger and watch her lovely body, her breasts heaving with each breath, but he knew they had to leave.

"Let's go," Jake said. "Get dressed."

They hurried around the room, shoving things into their backpacks and throwing on clothes.

"Who were they?" Su asked, confused. She put on her bra and then pulled a sweater over her head.

"I don't know. But I sure as hell don't want to hang around and find out."

Jake put on his pants and then his socks and shoes. While he was leaning down to tie his shoes, he noticed the gun under the table. He was about to pick it up when he thought about prints. Putting on his leather driving gloves, he picked up the silenced automatic pistol. It was a knock off of the Russian Makarov in .22 caliber. Small caliber but quiet with a silencer.

"That was their gun?" Su asked.

"Yeah." Jake pulled out the clip. Without counting, it looked to hold at least fifteen rounds. He pulled the bullet from the chamber.

"Why are they trying to kill us?" she asked him. She was now dressed and ready to roll.

Jake shrugged. "They have to be part of what's going on up north. But the better question is, how did they find us?" He had cut the handle off his backpack and checked everything else out thoroughly. As far as he knew, everything he had was clean.

"Why you looking at me?" she said, her head to one side.

There was nothing on her, he knew. She had never left his sight, so she couldn't have called anyone. And why would she? But how else?

"Do you have anything in your pack. Any way they could trace you?"

"No!" She looked hurt and disturbed by his question.

"I had to ask."

She put her hands on her hips. "What about the car? They would have found the man. His car was gone. They would know we took it."

"That's why I parked it in the isolated part of the parking lot," he said. It wasn't the time to argue about it, though. They had to leave now.

After unscrewing the silencer, he shoved the empty gun into his inside jacket pocket.

"Come on," he said. "They'll be back with their friends soon." He checked his watch. It was almost six a.m. and the sun was still a ways from coming up.

They both put on their packs and went to the door. Cautiously, Jake left first, checking both ways. He headed out down the corridor in the opposite direction that the men had gone. Jake thought about going by the front desk and taking care of the person who had given away their room, but he realized that just about anyone would have done so with a gun shoved up their nose.

Instead, Jake lead them out a side exit. They couldn't go to the car, that was certain. Hurry, Jake, think fast, he thought, as he glanced about the parking lot.

Then he saw his answer just as he saw a small van with blue lights on top, swirling about, approach from the road that lead to the airport. There would be more to come, he knew. Move it.

There was an airport shuttle van parked just down from the lobby entrance. It was their only chance.

Su looked nervous as Jake pulled her forward toward the van.

The van was empty except for the driver, a tiny man with hair almost to his shoulders. Su got in first, telling the man they had to hurry or they would miss their flight. The man, whose face was weathered, looked at Jake with suspicion, his cigarette bobbing from his mouth as he said something to Su.

She told him to get going, waving her hand at him.

Reluctantly, the man put the van in gear and pulled out of the parking lot.

"What's going on?" Jake whispered to her.

"He asked about the blood on your head. That hit broke open your wound."

Jake felt with his left hand, pulling back a swatch of blood on his palm.

"I told him you were an American kickboxer," Su said, "and you had another fight tonight. Here." She handed him a silk scarf.

"That was quick thinking," Jake said. "This is silk."

"Does not matter."

He wiped the blood and then held the scarf against his wound. "I was about to pistol-whip his ass."

Her eyebrows rose. "Pistol whip?"

"Pull the gun and knock him into next week," Jake explained. "Didn't you watch American T.V. at Stanford?"

"Stanford is hard. No time."

The driver pulled out into light traffic and made a comment when another police van swished past, its blue lights flashing. Su answered him and he laughed in response.

"What'd you say?"

"I said a young couple were having a fight, throwing furniture around their room. I said they had kept most of the hotel up all night with their fighting."

"You're good at this," Jake told her, whispering in her ear.

They got to the airport moments later and the driver dropped them off at the curb. Jake gave him a modest tip. Maybe he wouldn't remember them. But Jake doubted that. He was sure there were not that many Americans traveling in this area of China.

Once inside the small terminal, Jake thought about an immediate problem. He still had the gun in his pocket. His solution wasn't perfect, but it would have to do.

Jake brought them to a row of chairs against a wall of windows that overlooked the tarmac. Across from them was a ticket counter with three lines of people. It was much busier than he expected, and that would work to their advantage. They needed to split up, Jake thought.

Jake handed her a stack of cash. "Take what you need to buy two tickets for yourself. Pay cash for the seven a.m. flight to Beijing."

"But. . ."

"We're not going there. Change lines, and then buy a ticket to Seoul for seven fifteen."

"What about baggage? They'll want me to send that to Beijing."

"Tell them you have to go to visit your sick mother and were in too much of a hurry to pack anything."

"I'll bring you your bag for the Seoul check in, but first I have to take care of something. Go."

Once she left, Jake hauled both backpacks into the men's room. He waited for a man to buckle his pants and leave and then went into a stall with the packs. It was a chance, but a chance they'd have to take. First he pulled out a pin from Su's frame on her pack. Then he shoved some toilet paper down the tube. Pulling the gun from his pocket, he removed the clip, pulled the bullets out, and followed the paper with one of the .22 caliber rounds, continuing with paper and bullets until it reached close to the top. Then he returned the pin to the frame. Next, he opened her pack and dug his hands inside. It was mostly clothes, but he did find her cell phone. Setting that aside, he looked at the gun. With a few quick motions, he had the gun in a few pieces. Then he scattered the handle in one part of the pack and the silencer in another. If the pack was x-rayed, which he doubted would happen at this airport, it would look nothing like a gun. He put the firing mechanism and the barrel in two different locations in his own backpack. Then, satisfied, he hurried out to the terminal.

By now, Su was in the second line for her ticket to Seoul. She looked relieved to see him coming. But he said nothing as he set her backpack down next to her and went to another line.

Within a half hour, Jake had two tickets in his pocket. One to Shanghai and the seven fifteen flight to Seoul. Now, without packs, he went through security, keeping his distance from Su, who was four or five people behind him.

They waited in an area for a regional flight to Harbin. Once that flight was called, they moved to the Beijing waiting area, which was packed with people. Sitting a few rows apart, Su gave him a concerned look when she saw four uniformed police officers enter the area. They appeared to be looking for someone.

Jake watched them carefully, planning his next move. They were so close, he thought. They had to make it. He rarely reflected on mistakes, for he knew that he would never live without them. Those who purported to be without error probably never took a chance. And now, watching the police sift through the crowd toward them, he only had his training and his wits to turn the situation in his favor. Nothing else would matter.

CHAPTER 37

SeaTac, Washington

Special Agent Drew Fisher sat in the driver's seat of the Chevy Impala, his eyes fighting to stay awake. He had driven around the Seattle area most of the night, staying as far back from the white Trooper as possible to avoid detection.

Now, it was five in the morning and he was half a block from the Trooper less than a half a mile from Seattle-Tacoma International Airport. The Asian woman had parked her Trooper in a hotel lot, reclined the seat, and seemed to be sleeping, Fisher thought.

What in the hell was she up to now? She had been there for a couple hours.

Although he had called in his position, and had been assured by the Portland office that he would be backed up by Network agents from the Seattle and Tacoma offices, he had still not seen them arrive. Perhaps they were laying back. Watching.

Fight the urge to sleep, Fisher thought, his head nodding down and then jerking back up again.

Suddenly, there was a light tap on the driver's window, but it seemed to rattle the entire car in his current state. He shook out the cobwebs and went for his gun.

When his eyes finally adjusted to the reality of what was before him, he powered the window down.

"What the hell?" Fisher said softly. "How'd you get here?"

Her right hand on her hip and the other strapped across her chest, Special Agent Jane Harris shrugged as her brows rose. "You gonna let me in? This is Seattle. It's cold and damp."

He unlocked the passenger door and she hurried around and climbed in.

Once she was settled in place, Fisher asked, "How'd you find me?"

She pointed up the street a block on the other side of the hotel parking lot at an older Ford parked against the curb. "That's one of our Network cars," she said. "There's another one behind us five cars. Are you all right?"

"Yeah, why?"

"I thought you'd catch your backup hanging about."

"I'm tired. You still didn't answer my question. What the hell you doin' here?"

"You mean this?" she said, lifting her left arm slightly. It was in a dark blue sling. "Portland didn't tell you?"

"Said you were all right but. . ."

"Turns out the bullet cut through without hittin' bone. They stitched up both sides, patched me up tighter than a frog's ass, and sent me on my way. Fuckin' doctor wanted me to stay the night, but I don't think it had anything to do with the hole in my arm."

Fisher laughed. "Glad to see your sense of humor is intact."

"Hey, the bruise is worse. Where one round hit the Kevlar."

"Thank God you have some padding there," he said.

"Ah, and I didn't think you noticed."

"I'm a trained Network officer. Supposed to notice things like that."

They sat staring at each other for a moment, neither sure what to say.

Fisher broke first. "What'd our local Network folks say?"

"He wanted to know if they should move on Li, our Asian killer."

"I like the way he thinks. What do you think? Should we take her now?"

She thought for a moment, unsure. "I had to catch an Air National Guard flight in a C-130 out of Portland to McChord Air Force Base. Rode in a damn mesh jump seat. Almost froze my ass off. Let's see this through. We can always take her at the airport if she tries to board a flight to China." Pulling a piece of paper from her coat pocket, she unfolded it and tried to view it in the low light. "There are three flights to Beijing today. The first is at noon, and it goes through Tokyo. Second is a direct flight to Beijing. And the third goes through Hong Kong. The Network will have people undercover at all of those terminals."

"I'm guessing the direct flight," Fisher said.

"Good guess. Had the same thought."

Fisher's eyes tried to focus on his partner, but he was having a hard time staying awake.

She put her hand on his arm. "Why don't you hop in the back and catch some sleep. I got a couple of hours with waiting at the airport and on the plane."

He let out a deep sigh and nodded. "You wake me if she starts to move?" Instead of going around and closing two doors, Fisher simply climbed through the two front bucket seats. He curled up into a fetal position, barely fitting in the back seats.

Agent Harris slid from the passenger to the driver's seat.

"Oh, I forgot to tell you about Cliff."

"He dead?"

"Hell, no. He's like a cockroach. The bullet grazed his skull. Took out a nice chunk, but the surgeon in Seattle patched him up nice, from what I hear. He woke up singing like a bird in a cage."

"Really. What he give up?"

She smiled. "He encrypted the files with a five-twelve something or other."

Fisher rose his head from the seat. "That son of a bitch. A five-twelve encryption scheme is impossible to break."

"But. . ." She thought about that, leaning back against the seat and turning her head toward the back seat. "She got the password for the encryption scheme."

"Cliff told her?"

"Yes. Before she took off from the Eugene bank."

Fisher swished his head side to side. "It's a riddle wrapped in a mystery inside an enigma."

"Winston Churchill?"

"Right. A nineteen thirty-nine broadcast, talkin' about Russia."

She turned her head, her eyes on the Trooper ahead. "Somehow appropriate," she said. "Let's hope we figure out this mystery sooner than it took them. One more thing. Cliff was yankin' your chain about posting the files on the Internet."

"Had a felling. I didn't think Cliff was that stupid."

CHAPTER 38

Seoul, South Korea

The regional flight from Dandong to Seoul had taken two hours. As far as Jake knew, their baggage had not been scrutinized thoroughly enough to find the gun broken down and separated between their bags.

From the Seoul airport, they had gone to the train station and purchased with cash one-way tickets to Osan, some 45 miles south of the capitol city.

Now, Jake and Su settled into their chairs in a commuter car among a wave of Koreans.

Su rubbed her left wrist, which had swollen and turned black and blue, and was obviously giving her a great deal of pain.

"Hurt much?" Jake asked her.

She pulled her sleeve down over her wrist. "No. I'm okay."

The train slowly pulled away from the terminal and picked up speed. Shortly after coming to the surface, they passed through industrial areas and slums before reaching high speed in the country fields. At that rate, Jake thought, they would be in Osan in less than an hour.

"Listen," Jake said. "I don't speak Korean, but maybe I can get you some pain reliever. It'll help with the swelling."

Suddenly, Su's eyes shot up toward the front of the car, her face ashen. Then her head shot out toward the aisle.

"What's up?" Jake asked her.

"Nothing. I thought I saw someone I know."

Jake looked toward the front of the train and then back toward her. "In this car?"

He had been rising in his chair somewhat for a better look, and she pulled him down. "It must have been a mistake. He's from China."

Jake was going to let it go, but something had disturbed her, he was sure. "You need to tell me who you saw."

She rubbed her eyes with her right hand. "He was a bad man. He handle me."

"He was your handler?" Shit! That's all they needed was a Chinese agent mucking things up. He glanced up at his backpack on the overhead rack, which contained the digital camera and the photos of the Chinese test site. How could they know where they were? Something wasn't right.

Less than an hour later, the train pulled into the central Osan station and the two of them collected their backpacks and drifted off the train with the crowd, Jake trying his best to keep them in the middle. Su's eyes shifted around trying to find the man again.

Without hesitation, they walked directly through the main lobby to the busy street. Jake nodded to the lead taxi and the man helped them put their bags in the trunk.

He and Su got into the back and the driver got in and looked back at them. "Where to?"

"Osan Air Base," Jake said.

The driver, missing two front teeth, smiled and said, "I guess that." Then he drove off in a hurry. "I no go on base," the man said over his shoulder. "Not allowed."

"No problem. Just drop us off at the front gate."

Osan Air Base was located some five miles south of Osan in an area of sprawling business parks that had once been rice paddies. The area just outside the front gate had grown along with the Korean economy, and had recently been incorporated into a new city.

Jake, thinking back on his Air Force days, remembered that Osan was home to Seventh Air Force, with squadrons of F-16 and A-10 aircraft that could quickly respond to any attack from the north through the Demilitarized Zone. The base was also a major transport hub for Air Mobility Command, with daily flights to Japan and beyond. Including Alaska.

As they approached the main gate, with its arched entrance and reinforced concrete barriers, Jake thought about his old friend, whom he knew was still stationed there, since he had e-mailed the man just prior to departing Austria, saying he would be nearby in China but would not have time to swing down through Korea. But life was full of surprises. He hoped his friend agreed.

The driver pulled over to the right of the gate in an area used just for that. Jake and Su got out and retrieved their bags from the trunk, Jake giving the man a nice tip.

"Now what?" Su asked him. She looked nervously at the security police airmen with their M16s across their chests.

"Gotta see a man about a horse."

"Huh?"

"It's just a saying," Jake said. "Come on."

He led her toward a building that was still outside the gate, used to screen civilian contractors and visitors. Anyone who needed a pass to be on the base temporarily.

Inside, Su stood back a ways as Jake went to a window with a female sergeant in battle dress uniform behind Plexiglas.

"Hello Sergeant Jones," Jake said. "I'm here to visit a friend. Lieutenant Colonel Stanley Bailey."

"Is he expecting you, Sir?" the sergeant asked.

"Not today. Otherwise he'd be here to meet me. Could you please call him for me and tell him I'm here?" Jake slid his passport through the hole at the bottom of the window, which she picked up and viewed.

She nodded and then clicked a few keys on her computer, obviously looking up Lt. Col. Bailey in the base directory.

Jake turned and smiled at Su, who was nervously holding her left wrist with her right hand.

"Sir," the sergeant said, a phone in her hand. "He'd like to talk with you." She slid the phone through the hole to Jake.

"Jake Adams," he said into the phone.

"Hey! What the fuck? I thought you weren't going to make it down here?"

"Change of plans. I'm at the front gate."

"Be there in a second. Time for some brewskies!"

Jake smiled as he slid the phone back through the hole and accepted his passport from the sergeant. He slowly drifted back toward Su.

"Now what?" Su asked him.

"Now we take a seat and wait."

She laughed. "Just like our military."

They took seats along the wall to wait.

Ten minutes later, the door swung open and in rushed six Korean police officers, their guns drawn and aimed directly at Jake and Su.

CHAPTER 39

"She's moving," came a soft voice from the front seat.

Fisher tried his best to wake himself, but his head was swirling about. Sitting up, he straightened his gun under his left arm.

"Why aren't we moving, then?" he asked.

His question was answered with one look toward the front of the hotel. A small airport shuttle was parked and guests were loading their bags onto it, including the Asian woman.

"Why'd she go through all this trouble?" Harris asked.

Fisher thought and then got on his phone. He told the Portland Network boss what was going on, and asked that a crew process the Trooper as soon as possible. He listened carefully and then clicked off.

"You got a hunch?"

"Yeah. Could be nothing. They processed her house in California and the crime scenes in Bend and Eugene."

"And?"

Fisher didn't respond immediately. The revelation from Portland was difficult for him to process. "She's worked for us in the past. Before we became the Network, though."

"Great. A former CIA agent?"

"Double agent."

The two of them watched the airport shuttle pull away from the front of the hotel.

Fisher got out and moved to the driver's seat after Harris had moved back to the passenger side. He pulled out after the shuttle, but stayed far back. It wasn't like he didn't know where they were heading.

The drive to the airport took only a few minutes. The shuttle dropped its load in front of the terminal, and Fisher, pulled over in a taxi zone, slammed his hand against the steering wheel.

"Can you drive?" he asked Harris.

"Yeah."

"I'm gonna follow her." He slipped out of the car and started after the Asian woman, who had a small carry-on bag that she pulled behind her.

She went directly through the security area toward the international terminal. Fisher flashed his badge, keeping his eyes on the woman ahead, and was allowed to pass without incident.

Overhead, a monotone female voice called out flights boarding in English and Japanese.

Fisher pulled out his phone and punched in a number.

"Harris."

"Hey, we're heading down to the international terminal. Any idea what our folks look like down here?"

"They said you met them last night. The homeless guy and the couple, along with a few other Seattle detectives. Also, you should have two other guys on your tail from the Ford."

Fisher looked back and saw a head bob up above the crowd, apparently looking for him. "Got him." Then he glanced back to keep track of Li. He passed the United terminal Gate 28 with the flight to Beijing. The woman kept walking. "She's not going to China."

A man got up from the United terminal and started out after Fisher.

"Got the homeless guy," Fisher said. "Only now he's in a three-piece suit."

Again, overhead, Fisher heard the woman make a plea for passengers to make a final boarding at Gate 36. Shit! He quickened his pace to close in on her.

"Not China!" Fisher said into the phone. Gate 36 was just ahead. He had no time to call Portland.

The Asian woman went directly to the boarding area. The gate crew was about to close the doors, but held them for her as they processed her ticket. Then she went through the doors, which were closed behind her.

Fisher stopped outside the gate in the wide corridor, people flowing about him like blood in a vein, a deafening cacophony of sounds all around him.

Suddenly, a hand touched his arm. Fisher turned to see the Seattle

Network officer.

"She got on the Korean Air flight," Fisher said.

"Do we stop the flight?" the Seattle man said. "Take her off?"

Fisher thought for a second, for that's all he had to decide. If they took her now, they would have no idea who she was currently working for, and he didn't think for a second that she would give up her employer. But it was best to check with Portland.

"Keep the car ready," Fisher said to Harris in the phone. Then he clicked off and speed dialed Portland. He told the boss about their current situation and asked if they should stop the flight. The Portland boss came back with an emphatic "no."

Now they had no choice. Fisher ran back through the terminal, crashing through people who got in his way, until he got back to the drop-off area outside. He frantically searched for the car. Then he saw it fly up to the curb from around a couple of airport shuttles. He could see she was having a difficult time steering with one arm, so he went to the driver's side and forced Harris back to the other seat.

Behind the wheel, Fisher put the car into gear and squealed away from the terminal.

"You all right?" Harris asked him.

He didn't answer. He was too busy weaving in and out of traffic.

"I got the info on that flight," she said. "It's a direct flight to Seoul."

"And?" He finally looked at her for a second. She had her cell phone locked onto her right ear.

"That gives us twelve hours to decide what to do with her. We could have our people detain her in Korea. Or, we could have her tailed there and see where she leads us."

By now they had cut across a side street and were about to head onto Interstate Five South. Fisher powered the car up to speed on the ramp, the engine roaring to life.

"Who you on the phone with?" Fisher asked her.

"McChord Air Force Base Operations."

"Great minds," he said. "That's where we're heading. You get authority from Camp Springs?"

The Network was divided into two areas of operations-internal and external. Although the two of them were officially assigned to internal U.S. operations, they were able to operate outside the U.S. with headquarters approval.

"Yeah," she said. "But they weren't too happy about it. They said they have people in place also. They should be on the horn to McChord as we speak. The Air Force didn't know me for shit. They needed approval beyond my pay grade."

They were on the outskirts of Tacoma now, the traffic not very heavy, since it was the weekend.

Suddenly, Harris sat up into her chair and listened to the phone. "Excuse me?" Then she listened more. "You're kidding, right?" She clicked off the phone and shook her head.

"What's up?" Fisher asked.

"They got you a ride to Korea. Military aircraft."

"Just me?"

"Afraid so."

Fisher flew through the morning traffic and saw the exit ahead for McChord Air Force Base.

CHAPTER 40

The last few hours had been trying for Jake. The Korean security forces had pulled their guns on he and Su in the Osan Air Force Base Pass and Identification building, which, although was physically outside of the front gate, was essentially U.S. soil.

Lieutenant Colonel Stan Bailey, in full battle dress uniform, 9mm automatic handgun drawn, had been backed by half a dozen Air Force Security Police rapid deployment forces with M16s locked and loaded. It had taken the Koreans exactly five seconds to realize their error, backing out and returning to their vehicles.

Now, Jake sat with his old friend, Stan Bailey, in the waiting area of the base hospital. Bailey had used his rank, and, more importantly, his position as the tactical intelligence squadron commander, to have an Air Force physician x-ray Su's left wrist. It had been fractured, and she was now getting a cast.

"You got a tendency of finding trouble, Jake," Bailey said, sitting down across from him.

"I didn't ask for this."

"Korean security wanted to haul that woman off. What the hell did she do?"

Jake looked around. There was nobody in the waiting room but them. "She's a Network asset."

Lieutenant Colonel Bailey opened a folder on his lap. "I know that much, Jake. What do you know about her?"

That was a question Jake had not considered since they met on the train that first day. What did he know about her? "When you work with someone, you learn a lot about them."

The colonel glanced down and then flipped through a few pages.

Jake and Stan Bailey had first worked together in Germany while they were both captains in a tactical intelligence squadron. Jake looked at the rank on his friend's collar. If he had not left the Air Force and started working for the old CIA years ago, and then gone private, he too would have been a lieutenant colonel. Part of him wondered how that would be, and the other part of him, that which enjoyed the freedom to come and go as he pleased, was glad he had chosen his current path.

"You better look this over, Jake," Bailey said, handing the folder to him.

Taking the folder, Jake reluctantly sifted through each page, planting to memory all that was there. When he was done, he slowly closed the pages inside and handed the folder back to his friend.

"Well?"

Jake lowered his head. "I knew she had worked both sides."

"But she killed one of our agents."

"Yet, the Network still found a reason to use her again. Why's that?" Jake yelled out. He was losing it. He had to calm himself. Maybe he was still thinking about some of the ops he had been on, and how a couple of those had gone to hell. Although he had not killed his own agents, he had still not kept them alive. How culpable was he?

"Are you sure she didn't kill her contact in Harbin?"

Jake shook his head. "No way. I was with her. He had just been tortured and killed."

"I talked with Network headquarters," Bailey said, hesitating for a moment as he thumbed the papers on his lap. "You didn't send the photos you shot in the mountains."

"There was a problem with the cell phone they gave me. I got no signal."

Reaching into his side pocket, Bailey produced the cell phone Jake had been given. "This one?"

The two of them, Jake and Su, had left their bags with a sergeant who worked for Bailey. "You gonna do my laundry also?"

"We had to check them to make sure there were no weapons before we could bring them into our secure area. You understand."

Jake did. He would have done the same thing.

"However," Bailey continued. "We also found a .22 caliber handgun and a silencer, along with a clip full of rounds hidden in Su's backpack."

"Shit! I put that there. Part in her bag and part in mine."

"What about the silencer? Where'd you get that?"

"We were attacked in Dandong, China. At a hotel. Almost killed."

Bailey turned the phone around in his hands. "The phone," he said. "It's been tampered with. . . rendered inoperable."

Jake thought about running through the cold forest in China, and then ran back from the time it had been handed to him in China as part of the package from Steve Anderson, the think tank man. Who, other than Jake, had had access to the phone? There was only one person. And she worked for a Chinese cell phone company. Damn it.

Just as Jake was thinking of her, Su came out from a treatment room, her left hand and wrist sporting a new, lightweight green cast. She rubbed the cast as she approached the two of them.

"Thank you," she said, bowing to Jake and then Bailey, her eyes sparkling as if ready to cry. "Don't know how to pay you."

"Compliments of Uncle Sam," Bailey said. "Listen, we should get going."

"Where?" Jake said, confused.

"Our guys transferred the images you took to a computer. You need to tell me what in the hell we're looking at."

With that, Lieutenant Colonel Bailey escorted the two of them outside and drove them in a Humvee to a squadron secure facility. From the outside the building looked like it could have been administrative offices, but Jake was escorted through a number of cipher-locked doors and into a bunker-like chamber in the center of the building, with enlisted Air Force personnel manning computers and others listening through headphones. They had left Su in a waiting area in the front entrance. Jake knew that only those who needed access to this area were allowed inside. Rank had nothing to do with it. In fact, the wing commander probably had access, but the base commander, who was more concerned with running the physical dimensions of Osan Air Base, might not have access.

Bailey stopped at a station with a staff sergeant sitting in front of a twenty-one inch LCD monitor. On the screen, Jake immediately recognized the photo he had taken.

"What the hell is this, Jake?"

Jake pointed to the center of the monitor. "As you can see, it's dark. But here. That's about the size of a three-story house. At first I thought it was a large telescope. Then this here opened. Can you flip to another photo?"

The sergeant clicked that one away and brought up another image in Photoshop.

"That's it," Jake said, pointing again. "I think you know what that is."

"Sergeant Jones," Bailey said. "Let's increase the size and focus on this area."

If there was any doubt before, that was erased once the image became more clear.

"You want me to clean up the color and contrast?" the sergeant asked.

"No," Jake said. "We'll let the folks in Camp Springs take care of that."

"Zip it, encrypt it, and send a copy to Network HQ."

"Send a copy to Shemya, Alaska also," Jake said. "Colonel Tim Powers. His eyes only. He's the project leader and resident expert."

The staff sergeant looked at Jake and then to his commander.

"Do what the man says, Jones."

"Yes, Sir." The sergeant went to work.

Bailey patted Jake on the shoulder and pulled him aside. "Nice work, Jake. From what I understand, Washington has been trying to confirm knowledge of China's laser program for some time."

Jake laughed. "At least since the last administration let the Chinese walk off with the plans."

"Fuckin' goat rope."

The colonel escorted Jake out of the secure area. When they got to an inner corridor, Bailey stopped and turned to Jake.

"That Chinese woman. She's hot."

"Yes, she is," Jake said.

"You more than just working together?"

Holding back a smile, Jake said, "I can't believe you asked me that. Let's go get a beer."

"I'll take that as a yes."

Bailey led the two of them into the front waiting area. He was the first to notice something wrong. First, the sergeant he had assigned to watch Su was laying on the floor in the center of the room. Knocked out.

And Su was gone.

CHAPTER 41

Camp Springs, Maryland

When the American Intelligence Network was formed out of the former CIA, FBI, and other government alphabet soup, they had sought a neutral ground to establish a new headquarters for the Network. The location had to have enough room for new buildings, yet be close enough to the U.S. capitol. The powers that were at the time had selected Andrews Air Force Base near Camp Springs, Maryland. That decision would go down in U.S. history as one of the most brilliant plans ever. The Air Force base was already a secure location, with the president's fleet of aircraft based there. The airstrip also allowed the Network to develop even further its own covert air force.

The external operations photo analysis division was housed in what had been a secure bunker used by the old air force wing staff during the Cold War. It was not only sheltered against a nuclear attack, but was filtered against chemical and biological agents.

The manager of external operations,, or MEO, whose name was only known by the upper echelons of the Network, certain members of the office of the president, and members of the senate intelligence committee, leaned back in his swivel chair in a sound-proof office overlooking the photo analysts below. The MEO was only six months on the job, having replaced the first man to hold that post, Kurt Jenkins, who had defined the new roll before moving on to the private sector as a consultant with the conservative think tank, The Western Institute.

A strong and intimidating figure, the MEO still was not looking forward to this next meeting later that day. He held the photos from China, newly downloaded, decrypted, and enhanced digitally for his eyes only. It was obvious to him, even though he had not come up the ranks as a photo analyst, that the images were of a new land-based laser system nearly identical in dimensions and construction to their own system, although an older version that had been a prototype of the one they were establishing in the Alaskan wilderness. The secure call from Colonel Tim Powers on Shemya just minutes ago had confirmed his own suspicions.

Now he had no choice but to act.

♦

An hour later, in a park a few miles south of Clinton, Maryland, the MEO got out of the back seat of his Mercedes, dressed in running attire, told his driver he would be fifteen minutes, and wandered from the parking lot toward the trail where he frequently ran.

Glancing over at his driver, he stretched for a moment before heading out at a slow pace down the dirt trail. Clouds swirled above, threatening rain, and making the mid-day run seem more like a dusk outing.

In a quarter mile, he rounded a curve and started to slow his pace as he saw the two figures ahead. Then his slight jog became a walk until he approached the two men.

Also dressed in jogging outfits were the Chief of Staff Karl Oestreich, and General Wayne Boles, from The Western Institute.

"This better be good," Oestreich said. He had a cigar between his thin lips, which he tried to light for the second time.

The Network MEO, hands on his hips and breathing heavily, lowered his head to waist level. Catching his breath, he rose up to his contacts.

"It's what we expected," the MEO said.

"The Chinese have our laser?" General Boles asked.

"Yeah. We just got photo evidence from your man there, Jake Adams."

There was silence as the three of them checked the facial expressions of the others.

Oestreich broke the silence. "What about the leak from Brightstar?"

The MEO shrugged. "The Asian woman hopped on a plane in Seattle heading to Seoul."

"Adams is in Osan right now," Boles said. "That's some thirty miles away. Have him intercept the woman."

Oestreich swished his head from side to side. "No. We need to follow the trail. See where she leads us."

The Network MEO, who ultimately had the last word on the issue, was conflicted. "I don't know. If we let her go and she slips through, it's my ass on the line."

"I thought the DVD she had was encrypted," Boles said, confused.

Letting out a heavy sigh, the MEO said, "I'm afraid it's worse than we had expected. Our folks in Seattle, through a little more persuasion, have gotten more information out of that Brightstar programmer."

"Johansen?" Boles asked.

"Yeah. Turns out he had not only given the Asian woman the encryption codes, but he had sold her the entire schematic for our newest laser system."

"You're shitin' me," Oestreich yelled, moving closer to the MEO. "How the fuck'd you let that happen?"

General Boles got between the two men, a hand on each man's chest. "Settle down. Even more reason to use our free agent, Jake Adams, to take care of that woman."

Somewhat recovered now, Oestreich asked, "What'll this cost us?"

"Your job and a congressional inquiry if we don't stop this woman," Boles assured him. "You too," he added, nodding his head at the Network MEO.

"That's not gonna happen," the MEO said. "Send Adams after her. I don't care what it costs." He pointed his finger at the general. "You tell him to get that DVD and do what the hell he wants with the Asian woman."

The Chief of Staff looked around. "Jesus Christ, don't say shit like that."

"We're makin' sausage here, folks," the MEO said. "It ain't pretty, but it sure as hell tastes good when you're done. It'll make us all look good."

Oestreich drew in a deep inhale from his cigar before letting out a heavy stream of smoke into the damp air. He smiled before saying, "What about Alaska?"

"What about it?" Boles asked.

The MEO looked down at the ground and said, "We thought the shooter was our only problem there. Turns out he was the fall guy. There's someone else. We have a Network man there working on it."

"Plug these problems," Oestreich said, pointing his cigar at the MEO. "What else?"

"I've authorized another officer to follow the Asian to Korea," the MEO said. "The man we had undercover at Brightstar. He's on a military flight as we speak."

"To Osan Air Base?" General Boles asked.

"Yes."

"Great. I'll have Jake Adams meet him when he lands."

The three of them, in silent agreement, seemed somewhat content. As the wind blew through the trees overhead, the MEO left the two of them along the park trail as he walked back to the parking lot.

Over the Northern Pacific

Flying at forty-five thousand feet, the B-2 stealth bomber, calm as a soft breeze, cruised at five hundred and fifty miles per hour. The two-man crew sat side-by-side in the cockpit, and Network officer, Drew Fisher, lay behind them on an air mattress. Decidedly low tech, but not uncomfortable, Fisher thought.

When he had gotten to McChord Air Force Base near Tacoma, Washington, he was more than surprised to see the B-2 on the ramp taking on fuel. Fisher knew that the only squadron of the highly secret aircraft was stationed at Whiteman Air Force Base, Missouri, so he had to ask the base ops commander, who had met he and Harris at the operations center, what the aircraft was doing there.

"That's your ride," he had said. "But only one can go."

There was no question that Fisher would be on that plane. After all, he had spent the last six months undercover at Brightstar. Besides, Agent Harris had just taken a bullet to her arm hours ago. She needed time to heal.

At first Fisher had thought the idea was insane. But then, during the quick pre-flight briefing, the pilot, Major Andrew Cox, had explained the math. The Korean airliner would be flying at an average speed of four hundred and sixty miles an hour with a headwind at thirty-some thousand feet. At fifty-two hundred miles, they would get to Seoul in twelve hours. The B-2, on the other hand, even though leaving an hour later, would fly at closer to six hundred miles an hour at forty-five to fifty thousand feet, and make the trip in about eight hours. A good three hours before the Korean airliner. Plenty of time to get from the American airbase in Osan to the capitol city by an awaiting helicopter.

"You alive back there?" Major Cox asked over his shoulder. "You were snoring a moment ago."

"It's a sweet ride," Fisher said.

"Best ride money can buy."

"Yeah, four billion a unit."

The major laughed. "That's a bargain, Mr. Network man. Which reminds me. . . I hope you have a major credit card."

The co-pilot laughed at that.

"Didn't know they hired comedians in the Air Force these days."

"Hey, I was in during the Clinton years," the pilot said. "Had to have a sense of humor with that joker in office."

Fisher couldn't dispute that. "Hey, how far are we?"

"We passed the Korean airliner about a half an hour back. They, however, had no idea we were above them. We have virtually no wind, so we should trounce their ass by a good three hours fifteen minutes."

"Excellent."

Laying back onto the air mattress, Fisher thought about what had to be done in Korea. What would he have to do with the Asian woman? He had a feeling that would be entirely up to her.

CHAPTER 42

Shemya, Alaska

At this time of year, there were only a few hours of sunlight in Alaska. So, although it was early afternoon, Network officer Lance Turner and his Air Force OSI partner, Captain Dave Eyler, were still having a hard time seeing across the tundra along the western edge of the small island. They were both in forest camo, nearly fifty yards apart, laying among the small bushes. They could communicate with an earpiece and a microphone that wrapped down the side of their face.

Wind howled off the Pacific and over the three-hundred foot cliff ten yards away, so they could speak softly and not worry about their voices carrying more than a few feet away.

Turner had found the satellite phone after the last call had been made, but had decided to leave it there and catch the person making the call. It was the only way to tie the phone to the person.

There. Turner saw movement. He raised the night vision goggles to his eyes and the man came into view, moving through the low brush with purpose.

"There's our target," Turner said softly into the mic.

"Ready with the parabolic," Eyler whispered. He had a parabolic microphone hooked up to a tape recorder. It was a crude system, but it was all that would fit out there in the middle of nowhere.

"Let's hope the wind doesn't fuck up our sound."

Watching the man stop fifty yards away, Turner saw him stoop down for the phone hidden among the brush.

The call lasted exactly two minutes. Then the man started to put the phone away.

"Now," Turner whispered loudly. He slid his gun out of its holster and started to rise up from the brush. Knowing that the rest of Captain Eyler's Air Force OSI agents would close in from the backside and cut off the man's vehicle, Turner knew there was no escape. He crept forward through the brush with his night vision goggles down.

A few steps more.

Stop.

"Federal agents!" Turner yelled.

The man turned, drawing a gun. Three shots. Three flashes.

Turner crouched and returned fire. Three shots.

Silence.

Then came a voice over the mic. "Turner, you there?"

"Yeah, Dave. I think he's down. Hold your position. Car secure?"

"Yes, Sir," came another voice.

Turner moved forward, his gun leading the way. His breathing became louder, his chest heaving with each step.

"Damn it! He's down. Call an ambulance."

Rushing toward the man on the ground, Turner could see the blood on the man's chest. Next to him now, he kicked the gun away from the guy's hand and then holstered his own and kneeled on the ground next to him.

He had a pulse.

"He gonna live?" It was Captain Eyler, who had moved in, the parabolic microphone still in his hand.

"Don't know. But keep that pointed at his mouth in case he says something."

"Gotcha."

Turner put his hand under the man's head and then slapped him across the face. "Wake up, you bastard."

The man lurched up, his eyes open.

He babbled a few words in Russian; questioning the profession of Turner's mother. Turner pretended like he didn't understand. The man pleaded for help and then mentioned money and his contact. Come on, Turner thought, you're almost there. Then he brought up something and someone Turner was completely aware of, but the connection was not clear. The man was fading fast, though.

"What about Khabarovsk?" Turner yelled.

The man's eyes opened wider. "Speak Russian?"

Turner said nothing.

Closing his eyes, the man went limp. Turner set the man's head onto the grass.

Seconds later, agents moved in with lights, followed closely by two men with a gurney. The paramedics checked him over and started CPR, but Turner knew that would not work. One of his bullets had ripped through a lower lobe of the lung, and a second shot had given him a new belly button.

Moving to the satellite phone, Turner pulled it out from under the brush. If his hunch was correct, and he knew that it was, then the phone call could be traced.

"What was he saying?" Eyler said.

Turner looked up at the OSI captain. "I need to hear that tape of his conversation. Was it all in Russian."

"Afraid so."

Shit! Then he should have been on the parabolic. "Let's roll it back and hear it."

The captain did as he was told. In thirty seconds, Turner had the tape recorder on play and listened carefully through his headphones. When it was done, he rewound and listened again. Only when he was certain what had been said, he stopped and thought for a moment.

"What's it mean?" Eyler asked.

"It means I'm heading back to Russia."

"The only two words I understood were Jake Adams," Eyler said. "You know him?"

"Yeah. We've met. Forget you heard that, though. Come on. We've got a call to trace and then I'm off to Russia."

CHAPTER 43

The sleek, black B-2 Spirit landed at Osan Air Base at seven in the morning, taxied to an isolated hanger, shut down, and then was pulled inside and closed up tight.

Jake waited as the aircrew opened the canopy and was helped down to the cement. The two in full flight suits were followed by a third man who wore a flight suit, but without the G-suit and other gadgets. All three looked like they were dragging from the long flight.

Standing to Jake's right was Lt. Col. Stan Bailey, a serious look on his face. Bailey stopped the aircrew and started talking with them, while Jake came over to the third man.

"You must be Drew Fisher," Jake said, extending his hand to the man.

They shook briefly and the guy said, "Yeah. Jake Adams?"

Jake nodded and the two of them started walking toward a side door.

"I got a short briefing on you en route," Fisher said. He stopped and pointed his finger at Jake's chest. "I don't give a shit who you think you are, but this is my case. I've been following this woman for days. I was undercover for months."

Smiling, Jake said, "I'll let your finger survive this time, since you might need it soon. Now, you tell yourself anything your little ego needs to hear. I don't give a shit. I was hired to do a job. You do it with me or not. That's your choice. In the end, when you're layin' on your back with blood oozing from your chest, it doesn't mean shit who's in charge. You're still just as dead."

Fisher laughed and started walking. "They said you were a tenacious bastard. Finally, a truthful briefing."

Jake caught up with the agent, his hand catching the guy's arm and pulling him to a halt. "Listen, I'm afraid I have you at a disadvantage. I got a full briefing on you while you were in the air."

Fisher looked disturbed by that revelation.

"That's right Mr. Internal Operations man," Jake said. "You've never operated in a foreign country. Maybe that's why they let you come here. You aren't a known commodity. But let me tell you something. I've been working on foreign soil since your face was still in acne back in Kentucky. I'd call you a Southern Redneck, but that's both redundant and probably, in your mind, a compliment."

Suddenly, Stan Bailey approached, a hand on each of their shoulders. "You boys done comparing dick size? I understand you gotta get to Seoul."

The colonel escorted the two of them to a car used by the Osan OSI for undercover work that was waiting outside. Bailey drove them to the operations building, where Fisher showered and then changed into a set of civilian clothes that were exactly his size. Then they got back in the car; Bailey driving, Jake in the front passenger seat, and Fisher alone in the back. Moments later they passed through the front gate, got onto the expressway, and headed north toward Seoul.

"What the hell you expect me to do without my gun," Fisher said. He had brought his gun on the flight, but it was taken from him while he showered.

Jake turned toward the back. "You shouldn't need it. We're only here to follow the woman to her source."

"You don't understand. This woman is a cold-blooded killer. I think she cums every time she pulls the trigger."

Jake smiled. "Really? We might get along, then. The photos we were sent were not very good. You'll have to point out this woman for me. And when I say point, I don't mean that in the literal sense."

"You fuckin' putz. Who the hell do you think you are?"

"I might be the guy who's gonna keep you alive in the next few days," Jake said, turning his attention to Bailey. "How much longer?"

"Thirty minutes," Bailey said. Then he looked into the rearview mirror at Fisher. "There will be a Network crew from Seoul as back up. They'll see you, but you won't recognize them. They'll look like every other passenger."

When they got to the airport outside Seoul, Bailey simply drove up to the arrivals area and dropped the two of them off.

"You boys need anything, Jake has my cell phone number," Bailey said before pulling away.

Jake had been given a new cell phone; a tiny model that fit in the palm of his hand. He had made a few local calls to make sure it worked.

The two of them walked toward the Korean Airlines international arrivals area. They had about an hour to kill.

"Listen," Fisher said. "We had a rocky start here. I'm sure that's partly my fault. I didn't get a helluva lot of sleep on that air mattress."

Jake had heard he slept like a hooker after a six-John night, but the guy sounded like he wanted to save face. "Hey, no problem. The briefing you got was right, though. I can be a pain in the ass at times."

"At times?"

"Yeah. While I'm awake."

They continued on until they found the customs area where all international passengers would have to go upon arrival into Korea. The plan was simple. Fisher would sit off to the side with a good view of arriving passengers through customs. Jake would get the signal from Fisher and they would follow her from there. The other Network officers from Korea would follow them. The only glitch, as far as Jake was concerned, was transportation. They were supposed to hop into cars with the local officers, who would reveal themselves when needed. Since neither of them knew the local officers, Jake and Fisher were working in the blind. But Jake had one ace up his sleeve. Something the local boys would not know about.

When the two of them got to the customs area, there was already a crowd of people waiting for friends and family members to arrive. That would be a problem, Jake knew. There were only a few other non-Koreans waiting.

Fisher took up a position along a wall of glass barriers where he could see passengers come through the customs stations and file down a ramp through double doors manned by two Korean security officers with automatic weapons.

Jake got among the Koreans and pulled out a piece of white paper with the name "Kim" in dark black block letters and held it in his left hand. He put his right hand in his pocket and waited, trying his best not to scrutinize the others waiting there.

Soon passengers started shuffling down the ramp, pulling carts full of suitcases.

"Black pants. Leather coat." Fisher whispered in Jake's ear as he passed behind him and went off to the side again.

Looking at the woman he had mentioned, Jake ran the face through his mind. He guessed she matched the grainy digital photos he had seen at the briefing earlier that morning. Leather, he thought. That would be tough.

Jake slipped through the crowd as the woman came through the door, his sign prominently in front of him. As she approached, he pulled his right hand from his pocket and reached out for the woman's left sleeve.

"Excuse me," Jake said, startling the woman with his hand on her arm. "Are you Kim?"

Her eyes opened wide as she pulled her arm from his hand. She simply shook her head and quickened her pace away from him.

Jake turned and asked a few more women the same question, before he turned and started down the corridor after Fisher, who was now some twenty feet behind their target. Jake didn't want Fisher to get too close, since the woman might have seen the agent's face when he had tailed her across the Pacific Northwest. Or even at Brightstar.

What happened next, neither of them could have anticipated. Two men in plain clothes grabbed Fisher up ahead, and as he struggled, armed security guards moved in from behind. Jake, unsure what to do, passed Fisher and the scuffle, his eyes concentrated on the woman ahead. The others were on him just as quickly as they had scooped up Fisher. He tried to pull free, but it was no use.

Jake's eyes concentrated on the woman fading in the distance through the crowd, her head straight forward, ignoring the commotion behind her.

A real pro, Jake thought, as the police dragged him away.

CHAPTER 44

The woman walked confidently through the airport terminal away from all the commotion toward her objective. There. Ahead. Standing in front of a bank of computer screens looking at departing flights, was her contact.

She moved in next to him, her ticket out, and her eyes alternating from her ticket to the screens. The pass was nearly impossible to see; two hands sweeping down past each other. Then the bald man walked away and she kept her eyes on the screen. She would not look at the note here. Take a seat in the waiting area.

Nodding her head to herself, she returned her ticket to her purse and then made her way down the corridor two more gates until she reached an area with a departing flight to Hong Kong. She would stay there until her real flight was about to depart.

♦

Standing across the corridor at a table in a small café kiosk, Chang Su watched the woman sit in the half-full waiting area for the Hong Kong flight. There was no way she would go to that city, she thought. Not after making the brush pass with that bastard. She too had been trained to sit in another area until just before the departure of her actual flight.

She looked at the cast on her left arm and thought about Jake Adams. He had been so good to her and so good for her, yet she had been forced to deceive him and run like a rat from a sinking ship. Maybe he would understand.

Focus, Su. There would be no way to follow her if she jumped on a plane at the last minute. No way to get a ticket that fast. No way to be sure the flight was not full.

Where would she go? That depended so much on the buyer, Su was sure. And who would that be?

She would not have to wait long. A half an hour later, the woman got up from her seat and walked down through the terminal only four gates and strolled through the ticket agents toward the aircraft.

What? This made no sense. Standing across from the ticket counter, people flowing across in front of her, Su checked again the destination. That made no sense, she thought.

The woman was boarding a Korean Air flight to Vladivostok, Russia.

Su had to get on that flight. She hurried across to the ticket counter to try to exchange her ticket to Shanghai for one to Russia.

◆

Jake Adams, sitting on the cement bench in the small holding cell, shifted his gaze from the dank floor to Agent Fisher across from him. They had been there for seven hours and had not said more than a few words to each other, each knowing they were being observed through a two-way mirror on one wall.

Why had they not tried to question them, Jake wondered? They had pulled all of their identification and were probably doing a thorough check on both of them. What would they find? Not much in the public system on him, that was for sure. However, if they looked beyond the normal law enforcement channels, he could be in trouble, even though he had done nothing wrong. Nothing they knew about anyway. What about his new partner, though?

"I told you to pay those damn parking tickets," Jake said to Fisher, breaking the silence. He had to do something drastic to get the hell out of there.

Jake got up and went to the mirror, pressing his face against the glass. "Listen you fuckin' fascists, I'm an American citizen. I've done nothing wrong but buy your damn T.V.s and radios for the past ten years." He pounded his fists against the glass.

Fisher laughed. "You're a funny guy, Jake. Appeal to their capitalism. I like that."

"You got a better idea?"

Rising from his chair, Fisher unbuckled his pants, turned around and then lowered them to the floor and bent over, exposing his white ass to the mirror.

"Shit," Jake said. "That's gonna show up on the Internet."

Fisher pulled his pants up and tucked his shirt in before closing them and zipping up.

"Yeah, and I haven't worked out in weeks."

Suddenly, the door unlocked and swung inward. The first to enter was a Korean officer in a uniform. Jake expected an escort, but what he saw next surprised him. In walked his friend, Lieutenant Colonel Stan Bailey, wearing civilian clothes.

Bailey shook his head slightly before saying, "My name is Stan Bailey with the U.S. embassy here in Seoul. There has been a huge misunderstanding, gentlemen. It appears that the two of you were mistaken for international terrorists on an Interpol watch list."

"We're tourists," Jake said.

"Yes," Bailey said. "They know that now."

The Korean officer, not saying a word, simply bowed his head in shame.

"Well. Thank you, Mr. Barney."

"Bailey."

"Sorry," Jake said.

Bailey opened a folder and handed back their wallets, which the two of them accepted.

Without saying another word, Bailey escorted the two of them out the building into his car in the visitor's lot. They drove through the center of Seoul, the darkness of dusk and the headlights of cars swerving in and out of traffic a confusing blend of chaos.

Jake said, "What the hell was that all about?"

Bailey shook his head. "Bullshit. They were pissed that we had not turned over the woman to them. They had some shit on you, Jake, but they wouldn't tell me what."

"But why pick up me?" Fisher asked.

"We're not sure. Guilty by association, I guess."

"Where'd the woman go?" Jake asked him.

Bailey hesitated as he honked the horn and weaved around a small bus. Finally, he said, "Korean Air flight to Vladivostok."

"Russia?" Fisher asked.

Bailey nodded.

Jake contemplated that. Russia. He wasn't sure what he was thinking, but he knew that things were becoming clearer now. "Do you have her by satellite?"

"Clear as day," Bailey said. "We're sure she has no idea you slid a tracking device into her leather jacket. From what the guys said, that was one smooth exchange, Jake."

"Do we follow her to Russia?" Fisher asked.

Bailey glanced at one and then the other. "Not officially."

"What about the other signal?" Jake asked Bailey.

Fisher was confused. "What other signal?"

"Before you got here," Jake said. "We put a tracker on Chang Su. My contact in China. She helped me get the photos. She had broken her arm. So, we weaved a satellite tracker into her cast."

"I don't understand," Fisher said.

"Su took off," Bailey explained. "She has been a double agent in the past, so we weren't sure we could trust her completely."

"That's not true," Jake said. "You weren't sure."

"Turns out I was right."

"She left. We don't know she's working both sides."

Bailey sighed as he entered the southbound freeway toward Osan.

"What?" Jake said.

"She got on the same plane to Vladivostok."

"Shit. Are you sure?"

"Absolutely. Our guys watched her. She stayed back a ways, watching the other woman. Then, when the woman got on the plane, Su followed her."

Fisher broke in now. "Sounds like she was surveilling her."

"Right," Jake agreed. "When'd she buy her ticket?"

"Why does that matter?" Bailey said.

"Matters a whole helluva lot."

"At the counter, just before she got on," Bailey said. "Traded in a ticket to Shanghai."

Fisher had a look of incertitude on his face. "Why buy a ticket to Shanghai?"

"Two reasons," Jake said. "First, she needed a ticket to get past security into the international terminal." This second part Jake was only guessing on, but he was fairly sure he was correct.

"And second?"

"Second. . . she thought the woman would go to Shanghai. She was just as confused as us."

"That sounds hard to believe," Fisher said.

"That she knew where the woman was going?"

"No. That she was as confused as me. Why Russia?"

"I had seen the woman before," Jake said.

"Li?" Fisher said. "The woman I had been following all across the west coast?"

"Yeah. And she recognized me. When I asked her if she was Kim, there was no way for her to hide her recognition of me. She was truly shocked."

"Where did you know her from?"

Jake thought about that. He was close to eighty percent certain, even though it had been dark when he had pulled the mask from her head before his run through the snow.

"Russia," Jake finally said. "Her and a friend took me for a ride and got me into this whole mess."

They drove on through the darkness toward Osan.

CHAPTER 45

They had gotten back to Osan Air Base by five in the evening, Jake and Fisher both a bit tired and confused, and Lieutenant Colonel Stan Bailey with another surprise for them.

First, Bailey had brought them to an electronic surveillance facility, with dozens of language experts from the Air Force and Army in front of computer terminals, headsets on, and listening to the North Koreans, Chinese and Russians.

The three of them settled next to a 40-inch plasma screen with a map of the entire region displayed. There were blips all over the place, Jake noticed. Each contact was coded and could be called up with a mouse click. The colonel moved a staff sergeant away and took a seat in his swivel chair, directing the mouse on two blinking dots, one red and one white.

"The red one is the woman you know as Li," Bailey said. He clicked the mouse twice and a box opened in the upper right quadrant of the screen. Inside the box was a photo of the Asian woman, along with a description of her background.

"You know that much about Li?" Fisher asked.

Bailey looked up at a confused Network officer. "Yes."

"What about the white contact?" Jake asked.

Bailey moved the mouse to the white blip and clicked twice. Another box opened with Chang Su's information, along with a photo that must have been a few years old. The information stayed on the screen for only a few seconds, because Bailey clicked both off and maneuvered the mouse back up to the region with the two contacts.

"Now here's the problem," Bailey said. "The two of them left

Vladivostok, and are heading toward Khabarovsk Province in the Russian Far East. Jake is familiar with this area."

Jake thought about that, and it seemed like months ago. Yet, it had been less than a week since he had been in Russia for the missile launch.

Bailey highlighted a square section surrounding the two contacts and then enlarged that area. "Judging from the speed, and local sources on the ground, they're both on the Trans-Siberian Railway about two hours out of Vladivostok, with another ten hours to Khabarovsk. That train is scheduled to arrive there by midnight."

"Why not just fly there?" Fisher asked.

Jake leaned in and pointed to a spot along the route. "The rail line follows the Ussuri River. Cross the river and that's the Manchurian frontier. We sure Li isn't heading there to make the drop?"

Bailey shrugged. "We aren't sure of much."

"No, no," Fisher said. "That woman is a control freak. She'll place the DVD in the buyer's hand herself."

"That's why we need the both of you to head them off," Bailey said, emphatically.

"How the hell can we catch up with them?" Fisher asked.

Bailey smiled. "Follow me."

The three of them left the building, piled into Bailey's Humvee, and then crossed the base toward the hangars. He parked outside the same hangar where they had parked the B-2 earlier in the day. Two security policemen guarded a secure door off to the side of the main hangar doors, and Bailey parted them with Jake and Fisher at his tail.

The inside of the hangar was now in subdued red lights. The B-2 sat in the center as technicians scurried about, preparing the aircraft for flight.

Bailey stopped next to a service lift used to load bombs into the internal bay of the B-2 and other aircraft. Sitting on the lift was two black cylinders that resembled sleek coffins. An air force technical sergeant opened one of the rounded containers for them to view. Inside, there was padding, but instead of the white satin of a coffin, this interior was entirely black. There were tubes and a mask at one end of the structure. Both ends were rounded.

Fisher's mouth seemed to hang open.

The pilot who had flown Fisher across the Pacific came out from a back room, fully dressed in flight gear, and stopped alongside the coffin. "You boys ready?" the pilot asked.

"Ready for what?" Fisher said, confused.

"Where's the oxygen connection?" Jake asked the pilot.

The pilot leaned over and pointed to a receptacle near the head of the container.

"And you've done this before?" Jake asked.

Bailey took the question. "That's classified. Let's just say it's been thoroughly tested."

"Whooooh. . ." Fisher said, his hands up in protest. "You mean to tell me you put people in here?" He glanced over his shoulder at the B-2 and then back to the other men. "Then drop the bastards like bombs?"

The pilot smiled.

Bailey said, "That's the idea."

"No fuckin' way!" Fisher yelled. "Flyin' across the ocean on a Goddamn air mattress is one thing, but this—"

Jake checked over the inside of the container more carefully. "Let me guess. Altimeter chute release." Then he moved down to the end of the container, where he suspected the feet would go. "What you use to cushion the fall."

"You got a smart one here, Stan," the pilot said. "It's basically a collapsing spring. You hit the ground and this outer case pretty much disintegrates around you. It's made from a tempered Plexiglas."

"So all that's left is the chute, a few pieces of cloth, and a couple of fittings," Jake said.

"Exactly," Bailey said.

Fisher swished his head from side to side. "No fuckin' way. What if the chute doesn't go?"

"Then you'll never know what hit ya," the pilot said.

Now Jake was a bit confused.

"What's wrong, Jake?" Bailey asked him.

"How do you control this to the drop zone?"

"Satellite guidance," the pilot said, pointing to slits along the upper end of the black container. "Control fins pop out of here after it drops; GPS satellite controlled. Once it reaches the set altitude, the drogue chute deploys to slow you down, followed closely by the main chute, and then you're in a free fall."

"And trees?" Jake said.

"It could be a rocky fall. But there's an inside release if you get tangled. You pop this, take a look, and then release the chute. You're cushioned for a drop of at least thirty feet without the chute. Shouldn't happen, though. We'll aim for a nice opening. Low winds. You should be fine."

Jake put his hand on the colonel's shoulder. "The Network better have a nice chunk of money waiting for me in my account."

"Already been taken care of, Jake."

"You in, Fisher?" Jake asked him.

"Like I have a choice? Sure the Network will say it's entirely up to me. Then I say hell no and I end up in Duluth. Fuck that. How far is it to Russia?"

"About a thousand miles by air to your drop point," the pilot said.

"Why not just fly commercial?" Fisher asked. "A little beer and peanuts. Lousy food."

"No can do," Bailey said. "First, the schedule wouldn't get you there until morning. By then the Asian woman could have made the drop and boarded a plane to damn near anywhere. As you know, she killed a bunch of folks back in the States. And second, we don't want anyone knowing you're on your way. Somehow they found out you were at the Seoul airport. You could be tracked all the way into Russia."

"And we can't fly a military plane in without filing a flight plan and getting major clearance," Jake said.

"Exactly."

"But the stealth bomber," Fisher said. "Nobody sees us coming."

"Right," the pilot said. "We slip in, drop you two off, literally, and continue on to Alaska. Hell, we don't even need fly over rights."

Jake looked at the containers one more time. "These must cost a good chunk of money for a one-use system."

"They're a bargain," Bailey said. "We can drop a SEAL team into any location, they take out a target or capture someone, and then we set up extraction. It's what we need more of in these times. Human intelligence. Folks on the ground. Even our smartest bombs can't compare to that."

Jake had to admit that was a helluva deal. Yet, he wasn't sure he wanted to be a Guinea pig. Regardless of his old friend's recitation of the familiar classified argument, Jake had a feeling they would be the first to use these flying coffins. Chimps not withstanding.

CHAPTER 46

Feeling like a man in his own grave, Jake shifted his body sideways to keep from cramping. The idea of enclosing him in that human bomb, at first, had seemed quite absurd. Put into practice, the idea became almost laughable, and he wondered how in the hell they would lock someone into these contraptions for longer than the two-hour flight they were on before being dropped from twenty thousand feet?

The air force technicians had locked them into the pods, lifted them into the internal bomb bay of the B-2, connected the oxygen and heating tube, and then towed the aircraft outside. He remembered the strange sound and rumbling as the jet engines turned over; he felt the slight bounce of the craft moving down the taxiway; he experienced the surge of power as the B-2 lifted off; and then there was the almost tranquil sensation of cruising flight.

He felt that now. Like he was floating.

In the briefing before their departure, Bailey had equipped them both with cold weather clothing, helmets with communications, goggles, and, most importantly, his favorite handgun, the Czech CZ-75 in 9mm, with three extra clips. He moved his left arm against the gun now, strapped between his biceps and ribs. Bailey had also returned Fisher's 9mm Beretta to him.

Jake had no idea what was in store for the two of them. They had gotten briefings and words of encouragement from the pilots for the past couple of hours, but they had been silent for the past fifteen minutes. He guessed they had to be getting close to their drop zone.

He wondered how Fisher was doing one rotation up on the rotary bomb rack. Jake had explained that he would be the first to go, but the Network man had not been comforted much by that fact. He had gone screaming and kicking into the darkness of the pod.

"You boys still with us?" It was the pilot, Major Cox, on the headset.

There was heavy breathing in his ear. "Get me the hell outta here," Fisher said, almost out of breath.

"Maybe a little valium next time," Jake said. "How long?"

"Two minutes 'till the drop. Oh, one more thing."

"Not a surprise," Fisher yelled.

"Once you drop," the pilot continued, "you'll feel a stream of air into the case. That's normal. You won't be on oxygen anymore, so we had to have a way to give ya some air. It's awfully thin up here."

"What about the cold?" Jake asked.

"Yeah, you'll get cold for a while. But that's why we gave you those clothes."

Jake guessed the two minutes were almost up. "Anything else?"

"Enjoy the ride."

"Right," Fisher said. "That's gonna happen."

Suddenly, the sound of hydraulics moving echoed through the bomb bay, along with the gush of air. Then it happened. That sensation of floating was replaced by Jake's feet pointing downward, and he was lunging through the air in the position of an Olympic luger.

Seconds later, Jake heard a protracted scream and he imagined Fisher was also on his way.

Air immediately streamed in, cold and biting his only exposed skin along the outside of his goggles and mask.

Jake tried to remember the briefing. Dropped from twenty thousand feet. Rate of descent and terminal velocity, based on weight and gravitational force. Drag coefficient and resistance. Force equals mass times acceleration; Newton's second law of motion. Shit! Just hang on and enjoy the damn ride. Hope like hell the first altimeter releases the drogue and slows the descent before the second altimeter releases the parachute.

He didn't have to wait long. With a sudden lurch, he was seemingly pulled at his shoulders, like a giant hand grabbed him from the air and shook him before letting him go again. Seconds later there was another pull on him, and Jake guessed the chute had deployed properly. The air that had been rushing in was now a slow stream, barely noticeable.

Remember the briefing, Jake. What next? Then he heard it in his headset. The beeping came slow, seconds apart. Then the beeps increased. A second apart.

Just as the beeps became a solid, high-pitched sound, his legs collapsed, taking his breath away for a second.

The pod shattered into thousands of pieces. Jake found himself rolling around in a foot of snow, the parachute attached to his shoulders, pulling him slightly. He shook his head to clear the cobwebs, his eyes spinning around his new environment. It was as if he had just come from the womb into a cold new world.

He hurried to wrap his parachute around his arms, rolling it into a ball. Then he dug a hole in the snow and buried it.

Wandering back to the spot he had hit, he looked around at what was left of the pod. There wasn't much. It had been like dropping a light bulb.

His eyes started to adjust to his new surroundings. He was in a snowy field no more than a kilometer long by a half a kilometer wide. Damn nice drop, he thought. How in the hell had they done that?

Jake took off his helmet, returned the headset to his disheveled hair, and covered that with a wool hat from his pocket.

"Fisher. You there?" Jake whispered into the mic.

There was a slight grunt and then, "Yeah. I think I'm alive."

"Where the hell are ya?"

"I don't know. A field of snow."

Jake turned around, scanning the entire field in the darkness. "Can you flash your penlight once?"

There. About two hundred meters to the north, alongside the pine forest. He had missed the trees by only a few meters. "Got ya. Be there in a second."

Jake trudged through the foot-deep snow, lifting his feet high as he hurried toward Fisher's location. When he got there, he found Fisher laying in the snow among the remains of the pod.

"You all right?" Jake asked him.

Fisher turned on his light for a second, revealing his ankle.

"Is it broken?"

"Don't think so. Just a bad sprain."

Jake looked around and settled his eyes on the black cloth that had lined the container. He ripped that into long strips and then wrapped it around the Network man's ankle and foot. Then Jake helped him to his feet.

"Give that a try."

Fisher stood and put pressure on his ankle. "Hey, you do good work."

Jake helped him bury his chute and helmet. They were about to start walking when Jake sensed that something wasn't right. Maybe he saw a flash of movement. Perhaps there was a slight sound, like a crack of a twig.

Fisher started to walk, but Jake stopped him with his hand to his chest.

Then came the familiar sound of a pistol sliding a bullet into a chamber, echoing through the night air. That was followed by a dancing red dot bouncing about Jake's chest.

CHAPTER 47

Jake thought about going for his gun, but he knew the shooter could pull the trigger before his right hand reached inside his coat.

"Jake Adams?" came a voice from the darkness.

Damn. Jake rushed toward the woods, Fisher hobbling up from behind.

"What the hell are you doin' here, Turner?" Jake asked.

"What the hell ya think? Just like last time, pulling your ass out of the frigid Russian snow. That agent Fisher?"

"Yeah. He hurt his ankle in the drop." Jake introduced Network external ops officer, Lance Turner to Fisher.

"You out of Vladivostok?" Fisher asked.

"Yeah, but we need to get our asses in gear. Shit could be goin' down right now. The car's up the woods about half a click."

The three of them moved off into the woods following Turner's tracks back toward the car. They got to the isolated road, barely a one-lane track between the tall pines, where Turner's car sat against a snow bank.

"A taxi?" Jake said. "That's a step up from that crappy Volga you were driving."

Turning the key to enter, Turner said, "It's a loaner I found at the train station."

They piled in, Turner driving, Jake in the front passenger side, and Fisher in the back. The car jumped to life and they waited for a moment before slowly driving off down the road.

"How in the hell'd you find us?" Fisher asked.

Turner raised a small device. "I set the DZ by G.P.S. I was briefed you'd be dropping by. They didn't tell me how you did it, though. Didn't even hear a plane. Heard this weird crash. Twice. Never heard anything like it."

"I take it they had you follow the Asian women," Jake said. "Where'd they go?"

Turner's face was uncertain. "I found Chang Li in Vladivostok flying in from Seoul. She went directly from the airport to the train station-took the Trans-Siberian all the way to Khabarovsk. Had the pork and potatoes for dinner. No wine. I don't trust anyone who doesn't drink wine."

"What about the other woman?" Jake asked. "Chang Su."

"They related?"

Jake hesitated and then nodded. "Sisters."

"They in it together?"

Jake explained how Chang Su had helped him in China, and how she had been working as a Network agent. Then Fisher told him about how he had been tracking Chang Li from California.

Turner listened carefully before saying, "That Li is the one who jumped you in Khabarovsk, Jake. Her and her boss. I have nothing on that guy, though. No intel. I saw both women on the train. They weren't traveling together. Li was in first class and Su was in third class, among the derelicts."

"Where are they now?" Jake asked.

"A couple miles down the road. A dacha on a small lake. Very isolated."

"What the hell they doing there?"

"No clue. Now, hang on a moment. I said they weren't traveling together. When Li got off the train in Khabarovsk, the other woman stopped her. She looked pissed. That's when the bald guy showed up."

"The guy who nabbed me," Jake said.

"I'm guessing so," Turner said. "Strangest thing, though. "The bald guy kept yelling at Li. Something about an album. Where the fuck was his album. You forgot my fuckin' album. Strange shit."

"Can't help you there," Jake said. "So you followed them up into the country. How you know they haven't moved?"

Turner thought about that. "I was told to leave them there and pick up the two of you."

Fisher stirred in the back seat, leaning forward against the front seat. "You know the two women have satellite tracking?"

Looking in the rearview mirror, Turner said, "Yeah, that's why I'm pretty sure they haven't gone anywhere. Bailey in Osan said he'd call me if they started to move. Hell, it's after midnight. They're probably crashing.

It's just up ahead."

The car slowed and Turner pulled over to the side of the road, cutting the lights.

Clouds slid from the moon, lighting the entire area. Something about this place seemed familiar to Jake. "I know this sounds stupid, but this looks familiar."

"It should," Turner said. "I picked you up just a half a mile up the road last week."

"Shit."

Turner pointed across the road at a narrow lane that cut through an opening in the pines. "They went up that skunk trail. I drove along the entrance, crossing their tracks in the snow. Doesn't look like they've come out. According to Bailey, the road curves around and stops at a dacha overlooking a lake. About a half a mile walk."

"One way in and one way out," Fisher said.

"My thought also," Jake said. "Let's pull in and block their exit. There's no way in hell they could get around us."

Without saying a word, Turner cranked over the taxi and, without lights, pulled the car into the long driveway, lodging it behind a couple of trees.

"There," Turner said. "Now they can't even push it with their car. Heard they gave you guys weapons. So, let's rock and roll."

Before getting out, they discussed their plan. Without any knowledge of the dacha, though, their plan would have to remain flexible.

The three of them got out and silently closed their doors. Even though they were quite a distance from the dacha, sound traveled a long ways in the evening.

Then they slowly walked down the narrow road toward the cabin, the only noise coming from their feet squeaking on the packed snow.

CHAPTER 48

There was a light on in the small cabin on the lake, they could all see that much. To cut down on crossfire, should it come to that, they spread out to the west of the dacha. Fisher moved around to the far side toward the lake. Turner was in the middle and would approach the small wooden structure at the side. Jake would move lateral behind the cover of small pines toward the front door. They had done it that way because Jake and Fisher could be under audio contact at all times, and Turner, with the night vision goggles, would be able to see each of them.

Jake crept forward through the deep snow and was the first to spot the problem. Two men came out the front door, weapons over their shoulders, and lit cigarettes. What was even more disturbing, was their Russian military uniforms. He relayed that information to Fisher over the mic and used hand signals to Turner, who was now almost to the side of the dacha. But Jake was stuck. He had at least thirty feet of open space between his position and the front door. He'd have to wait for them to finish and go back inside. No, that wouldn't work. What were the soldiers doing there? Whatever the reason, they were in his way.

The moon was visible now, but Jake looked up and could see that the clouds would soon cover it again.

"Fisher," Jake whispered. "Once the clouds cover the moon, I need a distraction around the northeast side of the building."

"Gotcha."

Now, they waited. He didn't want the soldiers to go back inside. Better to take them out and deal with the others without the extra guns.

They didn't have to wait long. A band of clouds swirled in front of the moon, bringing darkness.

Jake slid his CZ-75 out from its holster and quietly slid a round into the chamber.

Then it happened. It sounded like a stick smacking a pine trunk. The guards immediately threw their cigarettes into the snow and turned to the right side of the structure.

"They're moving toward you, Fisher."

The two soldiers hurried around the side of the building and Jake rushed the front door, his gun leading the way. Through the corner of his eye, he saw Turner pull up alongside the west end of the dacha.

Jake slid up to the rough cut structure and peered through the edge of a small window by the door.

Then, the unthinkable happened. The moon came out again. Shortly, bursts of gunfire broke out from two AK-47s. More shots. But these were familiar 9mm rounds.

"Fisher. You all right?" Jake asked softly.

Nothing.

There was movement inside the dacha. Jake was stuck. They could fly out the door right into him.

He looked behind him and saw Turner at the corner of the building. Jake motioned for him to go around the side to see what had happened.

As Jake turned back around, one of the soldiers appeared at the far corner. Surprised. He started to raise his gun.

Crouching down, Jake shot once without thinking, catching the man in the throat. The soldier collapsed immediately into the snow.

There was more gunfire out back. First the AK-47 and then a 9mm.

Now came a haunting silence. Jake was shaking, unsure how to proceed. He had heard nothing from Fisher, and now Turner was gone as well.

Suddenly, the door burst open, followed by a shot. Having only a second to react, Jake took the bullet on the top of his left shoulder, twirling him around and back into the snow bank. He rolled to his side and tried to move his gun up into a firing position, when his eyes focused on the door once again.

Standing there, gun in hand, was Colonel Yuri Pushkina, his old friend and associate from the Russian Missile Forces.

"Yuri," Jake whispered. He let his gun drop to the snow.

"Jake," the Russian said. "What?" He stopped and motioned for the two Chinese women to get Jake.

When Jake saw Chang Su, her eyes were red from crying. She had a horrified look in those distressed eyes. The two women helped him up, Li grabbed his gun, and then they pulled him into the dacha, closing and locking the door behind them.

"Put him there," Yuri said, pointing to a wooden chair near the fireplace. He paced back and forth along the wooden floor.

Su and Li stood back and watched.

"What are you doing here, Jake?" the colonel asked.

"You said I should come fishing sometime."

The Russian laughed. "You see. That's why I like you. Always a sense of humor. How many friends did you bring with you?" The colonel stepped toward Jake and then ripped the hat and headset from Jake's head.

Jake put his right hand over the bullet wound, trying to stop the bleeding and hoping to dull some of the throbbing. There wasn't much blood, and perhaps that was a good sign. More likely, though, the bullet had ripped through his shoulder socket and would need surgery to repair. That was the least of his problems now, though.

"Good thing your aim was off," Jake said.

The colonel laughed under his breath. "Yeah, I was aiming for your head. You moved."

"Thanks."

"I had no idea it was you, Jake."

"Why?" Jake tried to sit up straight, but the pain was making him dizzy.

"Why what? Why not kill you in Beijing? Why not kill you in Harbin? Why not kill you in Seoul?"

Jake ran each city through his mind, his thoughts a flurry of uncertainty.

"You're like a cat, Jake. Nine lives."

"I think I'm down a few lives after this last week," Jake said.

"Maybe you've run out. It happens eventually."

Jake looked across the room at Chang Su. "You mean you could have had Su kill me at any time. That's true."

Yuri looked at both women. "They are extraordinary women. But—"

"But you wanted us to get the photos of the Chinese laser site," Jake said. "You could use that as leverage in case your other plan failed." His mind reeled now, unsure of his own thoughts.

"You're a bit too smart, Jake."

"You couldn't handle the Chinese having that weapon while Russia languished in corruption and military poverty. All of your power, your vast missile systems, would become obsolete. So you went out to some free agents." Jake hesitated long enough to get his breath and point over to the two Chinese women. "You had to have this laser system for mother Russia."

Chang Su was shaking her head, tears flowing to her cheek.

Yuri waved his gun around. "You're half right, Jake."

"Where's the DVD?"

Looking confused, Yuri said, "You know more than I thought. Your friends told you that?"

"I've got more friends than you might think," Jake said, his eyes moving toward the front window. "You don't think I'd come all the way out here without the cavalry?"

Yuri laughed. "Your American Westerns." He shook his head. "Jake, I think you might be crazy enough."

Before Jake could respond, all hell broke loose.

First, the front window shattered, a bullet flying in and catching Yuri in the stomach, buckling him to the floor and sending his gun bouncing across the oak boards.

Then something completely unexpected happened. Chang Su knocked the gun from her sister's hand, sending it across the floor toward Jake. Su followed that up with some major martial arts. But Li, caught off guard at first, recovered and sent her sister flailing across the floor with a kick to the sternum.

Su jumped back to her feet and the two of them locked and wrestled each other to the floor.

This gave Jake an opening. Still dazed, he flung himself to the floor and grabbed his gun.

Suddenly, the front door crashed in and Fisher was there at one side, his gun drawn.

"You all right, Jake?" Fisher yelled.

Jake rose to his knees. "Yeah." Then he started to crawl toward Yuri.

The flash from Jake's left surprised him, and he crouched lower. The bullets seemed to fly right over his head. The return fire came from the door. Three shots.

Guttural laughter echoed from the back room, followed by giggling.

Jake lifted himself up, his gun aimed toward the laughter. He fired six times and then rolled to his side.

Silence.

Then there was sobbing from across the floor.

"Fisher, you still with us?" Jake yelled.

He heard a grunt from the outside doorway. "Took one in the leg. Same one that I sprained in the drop."

Jake lowered himself to the floor and gazed across to where the two sisters had been fighting. Su was huddled there, holding her sister with both arms, and tears streaming down as she cried.

"You get that bastard in the back room, Jake?" Fisher said from the doorway. He had dragged himself from around the corner, and his head was now visible.

"Don't know. Think so. About time to find out." Jake rolled to his left, his gun aimed toward the back room. All he saw was a hand and a gun about a foot from that.

Jake got up and rushed toward the man, his gun pointed and ready to fire. He kicked away the man's gun and checked for a pulse. Nothing.

Jake hurried into the room, which turned out to be Yuri's bedroom, and checked for anyone else. "It's clear, Fisher."

Looking down at the man on the floor, he saw that it was a Chinese man whose face he had seen before. He was sure it was one of the men who tried to kill them in the hotel in Dandong, and the same guy from Seoul.

Fisher dragged his leg to where Jake stood. "That's the guy who kidnapped you? Li's runner?"

"Yeah. How's Turner?"

The Network man shook his head and then cast his eyes on Chang Su, who was still holding her sister.

Jake went over to Chang Su and kneeled beside her. Li's neck was bruised and obviously broken.

"I'm sorry," Jake said.

Reaching inside Li's leather jacket, Jake finally found the DVD, which he handed to Fisher.

Su let her sister's head rest on the floor and then wrapped her arms around Jake, her sobbing escalating into frantic crying. Jake held her tight in his arms, her head enveloped in his chest.

CHAPTER 49

Innsbruck, Austria

Jake Adams put his nose against the cold window, his eyes staring at the aqua-blue water of the Inn River flowing by. Across the water were rows of colorful apartment buildings with Gothic and Baroque facades. The snow from the night before left a layer of six inches in the city, but the mountains all around the city had gotten at least two feet.

Thinking back over the past two weeks, Jake had been able to piece together all that had happened. Su had told him how her sister had been working for both the Chinese and Yuri. The Chinese man had been the handler for both of them over the years. Su had assured him that she had not been working both sides; only with the Network. She had left Osan because she had seen this old handler, and knew he was still controlling her sister. She had to stop Li. Nothing else mattered. Li had disgraced her family, and she needed to save face for all of them.

The Chinese government, much to Su's dismay, was still holding her family. But Jake knew that would change soon. The Network had provided DNA and planted a story that both sisters were dead. The government would let the family go, but Su could never return to China.

Turner had taken a round to his head, dying instantly, and was recognized in a private ceremony for he and Armstrong back in Camp Springs, Maryland.

Fisher had been picked up by a private jet in Khabarovsk, and Jake heard he was convalescing his leg in Central Oregon, along with another Network officer who had taken a bullet in the arm.

Two hands came up around Jake from behind. The left hand, still in a cast, GPS tracker removed, rubbed his chest just below the bandage from his surgery to his shoulder, and the right hand came to his chest, the fingers running through his hair.

"You're awake," Jake said.

Chang Su put her lips against Jake's right shoulder and kissed him. Then she raised her head and nibbled on his right ear.

"It's so beautiful here," she whispered. "The mountains. The snow. The river. And you." She lay her head against his back.

Jake turned around and gazed at her wonderfully naked body. She was perfect, he thought. He pulled her to him and they embraced for a long time.

They kissed gently and then Jake placed her head against his chest. Together they turned and gazed at the river and the mountains.